NICHOLAS ROYLE has published five collections of short fiction, including *The Dummy & Other Uncanny Stories* (Swan River Press), *London Gothic* and *Manchester Uncanny* (both Confingo). He is also the author of seven novels, most recently *First Novel* (Vintage). He has edited more than two dozen anthologies, including thirteen earlier volumes of *Best British Short Stories*. He also runs Nightjar Press, which publishes original short stories as limited-edition chapbooks. His first work of non-fiction, *White Spines: Confessions of a Book Collector* (Salt), published in 2021, was followed by *Shadow Lines: Searching For the Book Beyond the Shelf* (Salt) in 2024. Forthcoming are another short story collection, *Paris Fantastique* (Confingo), and *Finders, Keepers: The Secret Life of Second-hand Books* (Salt).

BY THE SAME AUTHOR

NOVELS
Counterparts
Saxophone Dreams
The Matter of the Heart
The Director's Cut
Antwerp
Regicide
First Novel

NOVELLAS
The Appetite
The Enigma of Departure

SHORT STORIES
Mortality
In Camera (with David Gledhill)
Ornithology
The Dummy & Other Uncanny Stories
London Gothic
Manchester Uncanny

ANTHOLOGIES (as editor)
Darklands
Darklands 2
A Book of Two Halves
The Tiger Garden: A Book of Writers' Dreams
The Time Out Book of New York Short Stories
The Ex Files: New Stories About Old Flames
The Agony & the Ecstasy: New Writing for the World Cup
Neonlit: Time Out Book of New Writing
The Time Out Book of Paris Short Stories
Neonlit: Time Out Book of New Writing Volume 2
The Time Out Book of London Short Stories Volume 2
Dreams Never End
'68: New Stories From Children of the Revolution
The Best British Short Stories 2011
Murmurations: An Anthology of Uncanny Stories About Birds
The Best British Short Stories 2012
The Best British Short Stories 2013
The Best British Short Stories 2014
Best British Short Stories 2015
Best British Short Stories 2016
Best British Short Stories 2017
Best British Short Stories 2018
Best British Short Stories 2019
Best British Short Stories 2020
Best British Short Stories 2021
Best British Short Stories 2022
Best British Short Stories 2023

NON-FICTION
White Spines: Confessions of a Book Collector
Shadow Lines: Searching for the Book Beyond the Shelf

Best
{BRITISH}
Short Stories
2024

SERIES EDITOR **NICHOLAS ROYLE**

CROMER

PUBLISHED BY SALT PUBLISHING 2024

2 4 6 8 10 9 7 5 3 1

First published in Great Britain in 2024 by
Salt Publishing Ltd
12 Norwich Road, Cromer, Norfolk NR27 0AX United Kingdom

www.saltpublishing.com

Salt Publishing Limited Reg. No. 5293401

A CIP catalogue record for this book is available from the British Library

ISBN 978 1 78463 309 7 (Paperback edition)
ISBN 978 1 78463 310 3 (Electronic edition)

Typeset in Neacademia by Salt Publishing

Printed and bound in Great Britain by Clays Ltd, Elcograf S.p.A

CONTENTS

To the memory of Christopher Fowler (1953–2023)

NICHOLAS ROYLE

INTRODUCTION

POINT OF VIEW

IN JUNE 2024, when arguably I should be at my desk working on the final selections for this book, I am out walking. It is not by chance that my route takes me past one of my favourite Little Free Libraries.

A Little Free Library, in case you don't know, is a neighbourhood book exchange. Not all neighbourhood book exchanges are Little Free Libraries, but all Little Free Libraries are neighbourhood book exchanges. You might find one inside a former telephone kiosk, in a bookcase put out to pasture, or in a purpose-built cabinet outside someone's house. There's one in Highbury, north London, that is regularly refreshed with interesting books and, on this occasion, copies dating from 2023 of a popular and highly regarded weekly newsstand magazine that regularly publishes short stories (which is how you know it's not a British publication). My subscription to this particular title having lapsed, I avidly check the contents pages for the names of British writers. There is one, a notable one. One, in fact, whom I have previously approached for permission to reprint a story of theirs in *Best British Short Stories*. (It didn't happen, since neither the author nor their agent replied to my emails.)

The story starts promisingly. It's beautifully – meticulously

- written. In the same way that Lionel Messi knows where the goal is, this author knows where the semicolon is - or where it should be, if you're going to use it - and they use it a lot, to good effect. There's a simile in the story, for falling in love, that is so good I feel slightly light headed as I read it. The pacing is good; there's real tension. The characters are believable and therefore I become involved in their fictional lives and care about what happens to them.

The story is approximately 6500 words and for the first 5800 or so, the perspective, or point of view (POV), is third person limited. Then, following a line-break, there's a switch to the POV of a secondary character, for three paragraphs, about 400 words, and then it switches back to the main character again for the last 300 words or so.

For me, this is a bit of a problem. It's not a cheat, exactly. The switch and the switch back are marked by line-breaks, but there are similar line-breaks throughout the story. These don't look any different, but they are doing a different job. There's no rule saying all your line-breaks have to do the same job. Just as there's no rule saying you can't change POV. But in this story, from my point of view, it feels a bit off. Had POV moved around from the start of the story, this switch (and switch back) just before the end wouldn't have stuck out. But, as it is, it does. Do we learn anything important as a result of the switch? We gain another perspective, quite literally, but it's a perspective we could have inferred.

In *The Art of Fiction* (Vintage), David Lodge writes: 'One of the commonest signs of a lazy or inexperienced writer of fiction is inconsistency in handling point of view.'

In the case of this story, the author is far from inexperienced, and the switch, being a deliberate choice, doesn't strike me as evidence of laziness, but it still doesn't feel quite right.

I cross the story off my mental list. (Would I have kept it on my mental list if I had thought the author or their agent might actually reply to my emails this time? I don't think so.)

Mine is a subjective response, of course. Another reader would not have minded the late switch of POV. Whoever commissioned and approved publication of the story didn't mind it either, presumably. In another story, I might not have minded it. But in this story it just didn't feel right.

Do I get a bit worked up about POV? I think I probably do.

Is it important, however? I think it is.

In *The Art of Fiction*, again, Lodge writes: 'The choice of the point(s) of view from which the story is told is arguably the most important single decision that the novelist has to make, for it fundamentally affects the way readers will respond, emotionally and morally, to the fictional characters and their actions.' (We might substitute 'short story writer' for 'novelist'.)

In *Best British Short Stories 2024*, there are nine stories written entirely in the first person, one in the second person, seven in third person limited, with one in both first person and third person, and two in third person multiple (actually, one of these might be third person omniscient).

'Victoria' writes, on the blog of professional writing, editing and design company ServiceScape: 'Think of POV like a pair of glasses that you give your audience.' As a proud and lifelong glasses-wearer, I found myself instantly drawn to this analogy, which she goes on to develop. 'In order for them to see what you're seeing clearly, and in the best possible way to experience it, you need to give them the best pair of lenses to do that. Those lenses are the different types of narrative voice.'

Ailsa Cox mentions lenses in relation to point of view when she writes, in *Writing Short Stories* (Routledge), about Franz Kafka's 'The Metamorphosis': 'In all storytelling, it is vital to establish a clear point of view. In this story, Kafka filters most of the narrative through his protagonist so that, even though the author is writing in the third person, we endure with Gregor all the excruciating physical adjustments he is forced to make. The term "focalisation", taken from the French critic Genette, helps clarify this idea of viewpoint or perspective . . . Another example of an author depicting the scene through the *lens* of a character is [Katherine] Mansfield's focalisation through Bertha in "Bliss".'

Do readers care about point of view? On the whole, I suspect not. I care about it, but I wouldn't have been able to tell you, without checking first, that, say, M John Harrison's 'Egnaro' and 'Running Down', two of my favourite stories from his 1983 collection *The Ice Monkey*, are both first-person narratives. Nor would I have put money on 'Creases' and 'Mystery Story', two outstanding stories in MJ Fitzgerald's 1985 collection *Ropedancer*, both being told in the third person. It may be the case that Harrison and Fitzgerald made the 'correct' POV choices in those stories and that those choices are partly responsible for those stories being as effective and powerful as they doubtlessly are, but they're not memorable details, or, I should say, I hadn't remembered them. I don't know what that means, in terms of how we engage with literature, but I know from experience that one of the ways in which a writer knows that a story is not working is when it grinds to a halt after a couple of pages and the author finds that they have gone back to the beginning and started changing 'I' to 'he' or 'she', or 'they' to 'you', or whatever.

Looking for an appropriate short story to be dragged kicking and screaming into a discussion of point of view, I turn to my copy of *Anti-Story: An Anthology of Experimental Fiction* (Free Press) edited by Philip Stevick and published in 1971. What should I find in there, among lots of other great stories (it's an excellent anthology), but Julio Cortázar's 'Blow-up', source material for Michelangelo Antonioni's 1966 film starring David Hemmings and 1960s London, with Charlton's Maryon Park a strong contender for best location in a supporting role.

Cortázar's story is set in Paris, mostly on the Ile St Louis, where Roberto Michel, a French-Chilean translator and amateur photographer, pursues his hobby of street photography. In a tiny park at the tip of the island he spots a couple, or is it a boy and his mother, and who is the man in the grey hat? And who, for that matter, is telling the story? 'It's going to be difficult because nobody really knows who it is telling it, if I am I or what actually occurred or what I'm seeing . . . or if, simply, I'm telling a truth which is only my truth . . .' The narrative voice actually switches from first to third person and back again several times throughout the story, not with any intention to confuse, it would seem; instead, the effect is exhilarating.

Michel takes a picture and the woman protests, demanding the film from the camera and insisting that no one has the right to take a picture (of another person) without permission. Michel counters that this is not the case, in a public place (he is right, incidentally, although publishing such a picture would be a different matter), and while their exchange plays out, the boy runs off, 'disappearing like a gossamer filament of angel-spit in the morning air'.

A few days later, Michel develops and prints his pictures, creating an enlargement of the one taken at the tip of the Ile St Louis and tacking it up on the wall of his apartment. Over the coming days, he finds himself breaking off from his translation work to study the photograph.

The texts reprinted in *Anti-Story* are organised into sections described as being 'against' something: 'Against Mimesis: fiction about fiction', 'Against "Reality": the uses of fantasy', 'Against Meaning: forms of the absurd' etc. 'Blow-up', which appears under the heading 'Against Subject: fiction in search of something to be about', is fourteen pages long, and it's not until page ten that we read: 'I looked at the photo ten feet away, and then it occurred to me that I had hung it exactly at the point of view of the lens. It looked very good that way; no doubt, it was the best way to appreciate a photo, though the angle from the diagonal doubtless has its pleasures and might even divulge different aspects.' It's a story about point of view, then, about perspective. While 'Blow-up' is a perfect title for the film, in which it's only through enlarging his photos of Maryon Park that David Hemmings discovers evidence of a possible murder, it's perhaps not such a great title for the story, as translated by Paul Blackburn. Indeed, the original Spanish title of the story is 'Las babas del diablo', or 'The Devil's Drool', a term for early-morning fog, the symbol invoked to describe the boy's flight from the tip of the island.

By emphasising the ambiguity of the dynamics between the boy and the woman – and the man in the grey hat – is the author further fogging the plates or is he seeking to dispel the idea that of any real-life encounter between two or more individuals there could only ever be a single truthful account?

'Blow-up' lets us know, in its opening lines, exactly what we are in for: 'It'll never be known how this has to be told, in the first person or in the second, using the third person plural or continually inventing modes that will serve for nothing.'

NICHOLAS ROYLE
Manchester
July 2024

BEST BRITISH
SHORT STORIES 2024

BHANU KAPIL

STORIES I CAN'T TELL ANYONE I KNOW

A NEW FATHER, a youth of about twenty-two, can't pay for nappies. His wife has a broken tooth. The baby is crying. He leaves, and within an hour returns with £100. What did he do? What you're imagining is what he did.

A young woman lives alone on an island. It's not exactly an island, connected to the mainland by a strip of earth that's submerged at high tide. There's a reason she chose to live this way. One night, a man enters the woman's home while she's sleeping. In the morning, the woman has a shower as hot as she can stand it. Indifferent, she cuts the sharp, yeasty bread in half. A cup of lemon beer. The dog loops the brine.

A man approaches a girl of about twelve as she's waiting for the school bus. Can I give you a ride? No, I'm waiting for a bus. A few weeks later, the same man, dressed in a hound-stooth suit in pale yellow tones, pulls over as she leaves the station. Would you like a ride? No, I'm walking home. I could make you famous. A few months pass. An orange VW bug idles on the kerb. Is this you? The man, this time in jeans and

T-shirt, wire-rimmed glasses and sideburns down to his beard, proffers a photograph. An Asian woman is standing in front of a wooden fence in autumn, squinting at the camera. No, it's not me. Oh, I thought you were her. We were engaged to be married.

At the age of nineteen, I joined a matrimonial website for Asian singles. Cajoled, I switched my video on. No, I'm not remembering that correctly. I took a photograph of myself, naked from the neck down, for him to masturbate to. The part of me that's survived everything that ever happened to me did not, at the last moment, include my face.

A father escorts his fourteen-year-old daughter to the car after a group recital at her high school. Ensemble pieces, mono- logues. You're so fat. Why are you so fat compared to the other girls? The girl, whose body has developed fast, does not think of herself as overweight. What worsens her mood are not her father's thoughtless words, but rather the embarrassment she felt when the cast assembled for their last bow. In those moments, her cheap black leotard and tights, laddered now in places, were conspicuous in contrast to the emerald-green catsuit of the girl on her left, and the mauve catsuit of the girl on her right, a raven-haired beauty who was given the role of Secretary Bird.

At the age of twenty-six, the outer limit of youth, my mother stood before a glass case containing a jewel looted from her birthplace. She screamed: 'You took it from us, now give it back.' The guard on duty escorted her to the exit, pitchfork alert. Afterwards, mum and I ate cheese and pickle sandwiches on a crumbling wall above the Thames, which shone and spat below our feet.

A boy walks away from the girl he loves, pauses at the gate, then turns to apologise. At that exact moment, an older man sits down next to the girl, right there on the bleached grass of Hyde Park. The girl responds politely when the man, a stranger, asks her a question. No, I don't want an ice cream. To the boy, this scene is one of betrayal, evidence of the girl's lack of presence or intensity in their nascent relationship. *Revenge is a dish best served cold*, the boy writes on an anonymous postcard, in his signature loopy handwriting, before posting it with a flourish the next day. What kinds of relationship did he have as a grown man? Perhaps good, perhaps bad.

A nineteen-year-old man falls in love with a man who lives as a woman. Every morning, this woman wraps her bright sari anti-clockwise around her waist and tucks it in with precision. Stylish, kind, beautiful, the woman is well-liked in the community. That the man and the woman are together is an open secret. One day, the man tells his mother he wants to marry her. Only then does conflict arise. Only then is the man forced to leave his community.

I lack the courage to write fiction.

JONATHAN COE

SUMMER OF LIGHT

IT IS NOT a small thing to fall into a Venetian canal. The consequences can be serious.

In the film *Summertime*, Katharine Hepburn falls into the canal which runs alongside the Campo San Barnaba. The director of the film, David Lean – a notorious perfectionist – made her perform the stunt four times, and as a result the actress developed an unpleasant eye infection which bedevilled her for the rest of her life. The canals in Venice are not clean. They contain a number of ingredients besides water, including human sewage. *Summertime* was filmed in the summer of 1954. Neither David Lean nor Katharine Hepburn knew it, but thirty years earlier, an Italian painter had fallen into the same canal at the very same spot. Fortunately, in his case, the experience did not induce a lifelong ailment. However, it was undignified, and brought to a messy end an evening which ought to have consisted of pure triumph. The circumstances of his fall have remained unclear, until now.

The accident in question took place in 1924. Two years before that, Livia had learned that she would soon be leaving Onè di Fonte, the village which had been her home for the first seventeen years of her life. Her father had decided that there was no future for himself or his family in this tiny backwater, and announced that they were moving to Bassano del Grappa where there was surely more work to be found.

Later, after they had moved to Bassano and she had made friends with Serafina, she would tell her about that last summer in the village, the summer of 1922, revisiting it again and again in her memory and always referring to it as the 'summer of light'. The two girls would sit on the low wall which ran along the pathway above the river Brenta, and Livia would tell her friend the story of the painter who lived in the little house on the edge of the village and how he had seen her sitting by the fountain one day and how he had asked if he could paint her portrait, and everything that followed.

Since Livia and her family had arrived in Bassano, she and Serafina had become firm but unlikely friends. Serafina was a classical Northern beauty, with long dark hair, flawless tawny skin and an immaculate figure: already boys were swarming around her, but on the whole she did not take them seriously and made it her practice to flick them away like so many flies. She was a smart and quick-witted girl with a burgeoning contempt for the male sex. Livia, on the other hand, was taciturn and inward-looking, with her granite face and habitual silence masking a dry sense of humour which was known only to those who were closest to her. For some reason she had reddish hair and she had no idea what to do with it. After years of failed experiments with buns, plaits and pigtails she had simply cut most of it off and now wore it in a mannish short-back-and-sides. She was aware that she was not pretty, and was beginning to understand - although the full truth of it had not broken on her yet - that this was going to disadvantage her for much of her life. But she did not resent Serafina for her beauty. She valued her, instead, for the friendship she had extended to her from the day they met.

'The sun showed no mercy that day,' she told her friend, as they looked down towards the foaming currents of the river. 'I was sweating waterfalls. The whole summer had been the same but that day was especially bad. I was sitting in the shade by the fountain, resting on my way back from the shop, when the painter came by. We all knew him, by sight at least. He had a little house on the edge of the village and he'd been living there since the end of the war, with his wife and his son. You sometimes saw him sitting in the fields, painting a tree or a horse and cart or some such. I must say there was something a little intriguing about him. They said that he'd spent some time studying abroad, in Germany I think, and in my eyes – perhaps foolishly – that made him a sort of romantic figure. Of course I'd never spoken to him before and didn't mean to speak to him now but I could hardly fail to notice that he had sat down on the bench opposite the fountain and was staring at me. Not just staring but looking at me in different ways.'

'Different ways?' said Serafina.

'Yes, he kept leaning this way and that, so that he could view me from different angles. He was making no secret of it.'

'But you have to get used to the way that men look at you,' Serafina said. 'They do it all the time.'

'Not to me,' said Livia. 'Only the night before there had been a party in the village. A couple had been celebrating their anniversary and everyone was there, dancing all night. There was a boy called Flavio – a beautiful boy, I had such a crush on him – and however much I tried I couldn't get him to look at me once. It was as if I was invisible.' She stared across the river and repeated the word: 'Yes, invisible . . .'

Serafina said nothing, but put her hand on Livia's forearm and gave it a squeeze. It was meant to be a comforting gesture, but Livia did not acknowledge it. She continued:

'That was why I was so amazed when this man said that he wanted to paint me. Me! Out of all the girls in the village. He said that he wanted to start as soon as possible and asked me to come to his studio on Monday morning. He had a studio attached to his house.'

'Didn't you ask him,' Serafina said, trying to find a way to phrase the question tactfully, 'what . . . sort of painting it was going to be?'

'Oh, I know what these painters are like,' said Livia, who was not altogether unworldly. 'They can't wait for their models to take their clothes off. All those pious, religious paintings from centuries ago, all those Ascensions and Annunciations. It's amazing how often the women in those paintings are falling out of their dresses and have their bottoms hanging out of their gowns. But my instinct was that he wasn't interested in anything like that, and I was right. When I turned up on Monday morning I was wearing my ordinary clothes and he was perfectly happy about it.'

'And what was his studio like?' Serafina asked.

'It was so beautiful,' said Livia, sighing at the memory. 'I think originally it was just an old barn, but Signor Rollo - a very clever builder, our next-door neighbour - had changed it for him. There were these three huge skylights in the ceiling and they let in all this wonderful *light*, this wonderful summer light, and everywhere you looked there were canvases and sketches in lovely bright colours and at once you could see that he was a very good painter. A serious painter. These were not the sort of paintings you see them selling to tourists on the Ponte Vecchio. And there was a smell in there, I don't know what it was - oil paint or turpentine - one of those things that painters use. Such a lovely smell, I remember it all so perfectly. I was there the whole week . . .'

'The whole *week?*' Serafina was incredulous.

'Yes, that's how serious he was. Every inch of the canvas took him hours. And there were sketches, first, pencil on paper, before he even took out a brush.'

'What on earth did you talk about, all that time?'

'Nothing.'

'Nothing?'

'He never said a word to me. Nor I to him. For the first few minutes, on the first morning, I tried to make some conversation, and talked to him about the weather, and asked about his family, but he didn't reply. After that, there was nothing but silence between us. Every day. And yet it wasn't awkward at all. He was absorbed in his work, and I was happy just to sit there, enjoying the stillness, enjoying the light. Enjoying the . . .' She was too embarrassed to say the word at first. 'The attention. Nobody had ever looked at me like that before. Or since. Looked at me so intently. As I say, I don't know why it was me that he chose, but I was so happy that he did. It was the best experience of my life.'

She stared ahead of her, lost in sightless reminiscence.

'And then,' Serafina asked, 'what did you think of the painting, when you saw it?'

'It was very fine,' said Livia, coming back to earth and choosing her words carefully. 'Very faithful. He caught me - almost to perfection, you might say. It wasn't a flattering portrait, by any means, but it was . . . honest. I liked his honesty, very much. But, to tell you the truth, I only saw it very briefly, when it was finished. Soon afterwards we moved here to Bassano, and I never saw the painter again, and I don't know what happened to the picture. Perhaps he sold it to a private collector, and it will be hanging in the dining room of some dingy villa for the next fifty years. Isn't that what happens?' Livia sighed. 'I would give anything to see it again, you know. Even a glimpse. Anything at all.'

A few months went by. Livia found work at a dressmaker's in the Via Brocchi, while Serafina continued to wait tables at a restaurant, the Gallo d'Oro. She began to attract the attentions of one customer in particular, a handsome youth called Andrea who had just returned from law school and was now assisting the local magistrate. He dined at the restaurant every evening and soon began taking Serafina out and before long everyone was talking about them as if they were a couple.

Andrea had a friend, Riccardo, the son of a wealthy factory owner. He didn't seem to work for a living, and kept telling people that he was going to join the army although there was little sign of it happening. Instead he just seemed to follow Andrea around everywhere, and was generally considered to be rather stupid and a bit of a pain. Livia in particular disliked him. But because he spent so much time with Andrea, and Andrea spent so much time with Serafina, she always seemed to end up in his company.

One day after work she went to the Gallo d'Oro and found, inevitably, that Andrea and Riccardo were already there, dining together. While they were waiting for their pasta to be served, Andrea was reading the newspaper and Riccardo was cleaning his fingernails with his teeth. As usual he ignored Livia when she arrived: he did not consider her pretty enough to talk to, even though he was no great looker himself. Anyway, this evening Livia had something else to distract her. She gasped when she saw the photograph in Andrea's newspaper, and snatched it off him.

'Look at this!' she said.

'What about it?' asked Serafina, coming over.

'Here – this is him! The painter from Onè di Fonte, my home town!'

Sure enough, there was a small article about the painter, under the headline 'Local artist will be showing his work at the Biennale this year.'

'This year?' said Serafina. 'In Venice? That settles it. We're going!'

On the opening night of that year's Biennale, 31st March 1924, the Italian pavilion was of course crowded. Livia, Serafina, Andrea and Riccardo had arrived by train and vaporetto. Livia was wearing her very best clothes but even so she felt conspicuous and shabby beside the hordes of elegant women in their beaded evening dresses and long strings of pearls. There seemed to be hundreds of men in dark suits, standing around in groups of four or five, chatting, smoking – doing everything, in fact, apart from looking at the paintings on the walls, which in any case were difficult even to glimpse through the densely packed throng of visitors.

An officious man in full dinner suit approached them and said 'Can I help you?' in a menacing way. He had been watching them for some time and had decided that they either needed assistance or – more likely – had come to the wrong place and should be quietly escorted from the premises.

'We're looking for a painting called . . .' Livia turned to Serafina with a helpless look and admitted: 'I don't know what it's called.'

'*Portrait of Livia*, I expect,' said her friend. But at that moment Livia noticed someone a few metres away on the other side of the salon. It was the painter himself, standing at the centre of an adoring circle of admirers – five men and three women – and holding forth on some subject or other with great authority while his audience hung on every word. Remembering the week they had spent together during that long summer almost two years ago – the strange, silent intimacy they had forged in his light-filled studio – Livia felt an overwhelming urge to talk to him now. She caught his eye and he briefly returned her gaze but didn't seem to recognise her, and so she was obliged to loiter on the edge of the circle for what seemed like aeons, unable to step forward, unwilling to step back. How much time passed in this excruciating manner she could not have said, but she remained fixed to the spot until she suddenly felt Serafina grab her by the arm and try to propel her away. She turned to ask her friend what she was doing and was astonished to see her face: livid with fury and contorted into the fiercest scowl.

'Come on,' Serafina said. 'We're leaving.'

'What about the portrait? Did you find it?'

'Forget it. Let's go.'

But then, above the hum of conversation, Livia heard laughter. She heard the voices of Andrea and Riccardo as they cackled and guffawed together. Breaking free of Serafina, she pushed forward through the crowd and found them standing in front of her portrait.

On seeing the painting again, she stood back to contemplate it for a moment. It was just as she remembered. Livia's eye was untrained but her instinct was good, and she could see that in its detail, in its brushwork, in its patterning of light and shade, this was a masterful composition.

'It's a wonderful picture,' she said to them, annoyed. 'What are you laughing at?'

'Oh, yes,' Andrea said. 'Quite wonderful.' He turned to Riccardo and spluttered with mirth. 'An exquisite study in the absence of beauty.'

'A paean to plainness,' Riccardo said, with a horrible chuckle. 'A triumphant *hommage* to the hideous.'

Livia did not know what they were talking about. Then she looked down to the bottom of the frame, at the little golden plate where the title of the painting was engraved, and her heart stopped beating.

He had called it *The Ugly Girl*.

Eventually Serafina found her friend sitting on a bench in the Giardini della Biennale. She had her head in her hands, her fingers hiding her face. It took half an hour to persuade her to say anything, and another half an hour to get her to move. Then for the next two hours they walked through the streets of Venice: past the Arsenale, through San Marco and across the Accademia bridge until they reached the Dorsoduro.

Serafina did most of the talking. She railed against men and told Livia that they were all idiots and she was going to split up with Andrea because he was an idiot too. She did everything she could to make Livia laugh, and when they finally sat down to eat in a little osteria in the Campo San Barnaba she told her that anyway in her eyes she was beautiful, the most beautiful girl in the whole of Bassano del Grappa, and by the time they had finished their second bottle of wine Livia was starting to feel better and starting to believe her. Her eyes shone with tears but they were different tears now, tears of gratitude.

At eleven o'clock they realised it was time to go home. But as they left the little restaurant and hurried across the square towards the Ponte dei Pugni, they saw him again.

At a more expensive restaurant on the same square, the Quattro Venti - one of the best in Venice - the painter and his companions were coming to the end of an excellent meal. The guest of honour had been the Baron Dieudonné Sylvestre de Montmorency-Noailles, a famously wealthy and discerning collector from Paris, who had been deeply impressed by the works he had seen on display in the Italian pavilion. Sales were promised. Further exhibitions were mooted. Everyone was in a thoroughly good mood. As the meal concluded with cigars and *grappa* (the best that Bassano could supply), the air was thick not just with smoke but with the oaky scents of money, success and entitlement.

A few minutes later, the dinner party emerged from the restaurant and wandered over towards the canal, still chatting and laughing. The artist never moved far from the collector's side. Together, they stood at the very edge of the water, which lay green and opaque in the lamplight, too thick and too dull to offer anything but the faintest reflection of the crescent moon. The two men conversed murmurously beneath the immensity of the Venetian sky. The collector proffered a witticism and the painter was heard to give an obsequious laugh.

At that moment, from the shadows within the doorway

of the Chiesa di San Barnaba, two women ran towards them. One of them had long dark hair and the other had short reddish hair. The dark-haired woman ran directly up to the painter and looked him straight in the eye and said to him, with great emphasis:

'You stupid prick!'

Some say that she ran towards him so quickly that he stepped backwards in surprise and simply lost his balance. Others say that, on pronouncing the third word, the dark-haired woman reached out towards the painter's chest and gave him a violent push. Whatever the truth of the matter, these things are certain: he fell, his body flipped back into a perfect forty-five degree angle, his feet left the ground, he described a brief, graceful arc and two seconds later, following an almighty splash, he was thrashing and floundering in the filthy water and screaming for help.

Help came swiftly. The Baron himself did not intervene, but two of the other diners wasted no time in reaching their arms out towards the unfortunate artist and pulling him onto dry land where for the next few minutes he sat looking around him in a state of absolute stupefaction. The taste of brackish canal water was rancid in his throat, his wet clothes stuck to his body like an icy flannel, and his mouth kept opening and closing like the mouth of a goldfish.

The others looked on, having no idea what had just happened or what they should say about it. The square was otherwise empty, and a curious silence hung over the whole scene. It was a silence broken only by one, receding sound: in the distance could be heard the footsteps of two young women, running to catch the last train to Bassano del Grappa, their progress through the narrow streets impeded only by the fact that they were attempting to run arm-in-arm, and kept collapsing into fits of shrieking laughter.

Nino Springolo's painting Ragazza Brutta (1922) *currently hangs in the Ca' Pesaro gallery in Venice.*

PAUL BROWNSEY

MANOEUVRES

HE HAD STAYED overnight at his mother's to make sure she got her morning train down to England and the relative safety of his sister's house near Crewe while the war scare lasted, and after that he was getting milk and bread for us plus the courgettes I needed for the courgette bake I was going to cook that evening. Even so he was a lot later coming home than I'd expected.

'Where've you been?' But the canary-yellow armband of yellow electrical tape on his jerkin told me.

'Maryhill Burgh Hall.' He spoke as though something totally ordinary were involved, like going to the dentist. 'Where's my framed rucksack?'

'You're not *really* . . .' I couldn't finish it. In any case, it was best to appear to play along with him, so I said, 'It's in the basement. I know where it is. I'll get it.' Drummond and I have – no, had – one floor of a large old house in Glasgow's West End that had been converted into flats. The basement was too small and low to be converted into a garden flat so it became a sort of lumber room for the owners of the flats above.

But instead of going to fetch it, I said in what could have passed for an admiring voice, 'So what decided you?'

'Didn't you listen to the news?' Having carefully put the shopping away in the fridge and breadbin, he was now rooting around in the under-sink cupboard.

'I haven't. It just leaves me so—' I couldn't finish that in a way he wouldn't despise, and already I knew, like a cloud of filthy grease engulfing me, that he regarded his husband as a selfish coward.

'They've landed. At Helensburgh. They've surrounded Faslane and a huge convoy is heading towards Glasgow.'

'What can you do?' I hoped I sounded interested, pronouncing 'you' so it didn't refer to him specifically.

'Stop them.'

'Can you? I mean, isn't this a bit, well . . .' I was going to say, '*Dad's Army?*' but I didn't want to get his back up. 'I mean, volunteer soldiers against a professional army . . .'

'Regulars are setting up a blockade at Dumbarton and we'll join them once we've had some training. We start training tonight. Battlefield rifles and anti-tank missiles. Anyway . . .' That word was not a precursor to further attempts to defend his decision but an intimation that he had too much to do to waste time talking. Having got from the under-sink cupboard the water-bottle that he clutches on his runs, he headed off to our bedroom, where I heard him opening drawers. But the fact that he hadn't stayed to listen to any more from me was encouraging. Perhaps he was afraid to hear it. Perhaps he wanted to be persuaded to give up.

I followed him in. He was sorting underpants on the bed. At least my Drummond would do what he could to maintain personal hygiene during the travails of war. My best weapon was his sense of responsibility to others. During the early days of the pandemic, when supermarkets were running out of all sorts of things, rice, bread, toilet rolls, tins of tomatoes, flour, he'd refused to stockpile, saying, 'We shouldn't take more than our fair share,' and I'd hid the stuff I bought in the basement. Now I said, 'I'm going to get the rucksack, but, look, you're fifty-nine. Yes, you don't look it, you're trim, not overweight, but the arthritis in your knees . . . You could hinder the effort, be a liability. Go and point that out to them. They won't want you then. Other people could die helping you because you're not so agile.' I realised that I was saying that I wouldn't be one of the ones helping him.

'If it comes to that, the solution's clear. I hope by then I'll have done something to keep the bastards back,' he said. I noted there was no emphasis on 'I'll' that could have implied a contrast with running-from-responsibility me. I'm happy to put on record that in all our exchanges that day, he never expressed contempt for me. But the simple determination in his voice to fight gave me a different line of attack. 'Isn't this the macho response? "I'm a man so I fight." Basically, male violence. Toxic masculinity. Fists, clubs, Kalashnikovs.'

'They're not Kalashnikovs. They're AX-something-or-other; I can't remember.' He seemed ashamed he'd forgotten, and I filed another possible manoeuvre: suggest he might forget his weapons training, too, not take things in as readily as a younger man, and so be a further hindrance to his fellow fighters.

I said, 'Okay, but I mean, there are bound to be diplomatic moves and the Americans won't be backward to bring some heavy-duty diplomatic pressure to stop Scotland becoming a base for them.'

He didn't reply, not even to point out, as I'd have done in his place, that volunteering to fight in a defensive war isn't the same as male violence against women and just beating up other people for the hell of it. Which suggested he was weakening. I switched to another weapon to drive things home.

'Is it worth wasting men and resources trying to stop them getting to Glasgow?' He'd started sorting T-shirts, which smelled clean and fresh even from where I stood, but halted and stared. 'I mean,' I said, 'they've got an interest in not damaging Scotland. That statement they put out last week.'

They'd announced they had no plans to invade, only to 'negotiate the voluntary grant of a purely defensive base in a beautiful country where the dream of free nationhood is alive again'.

I said, 'Sounds like they're counting on nationalist feeling to support them against the UK. Hinting at a promise of independence in return for collusion. Co-operation. People are not going to co-operate if they reduce Glasgow to another Mariupol.'

Or maybe, I suddenly thought, they'll destroy Glasgow to make clear the penalty for non-collusion.

'A stand needs to be made and it's not for me to decide where.' Suddenly there was ferocity in his voice, as though he was challenging a lot more than dubious speculation about how far Scotland could be wedged away from the UK, so I backed off into, 'I think your rucksack is in behind that pile of garden furniture we got when your mother downsized.' That was a mistake because now that he knew where it was, I couldn't delay him on the basis that only I knew where it was. To stop him going down to get it himself, I said, 'Who knows, though? It could be anywhere,' and that was a mistake, too, because if I didn't know where it was any more than he did, he had a different reason not to wait for me to fetch it but to go chasing down to the basement himself. Because of these mistakes, I lurched into another line more clumsily than I'd intended. 'You know, you are so atomic.' Then I attempted a laugh, like I was joshing him on one of his most lovable features.

'Atomic?' He looked up from separating his socks from my socks out of a pile that had been washed together. Rather symbolic, but nice that he was being so careful not to make off with any of my socks. 'Is that some kind of joke?' The voice could have been threatening.

'Joke?'

'To do with the fact that they've surrounded the British nuclear submarine base at Faslane?'

'No.' I dragged out the word comfortingly, making it absolutely clear I wasn't joking about a thing like that. 'But, see, it's like when you gave up your teaching job – yes, I know you hated it – and enrolled to retrain in IT, and you did it all before you told me. Living together, joint bank account, joint mortgage, but not something to discuss with me. So you were atomic, i.e. not part of a molecule. And I'd have supported your decision. I would. But I mean, don't you think becoming a volunteer soldier and probably getting yourself killed was something to sort of, you know, like, mention to your husband, if only, like, in passing, before you did it?' I laughed again.

He gave me what they call a black look, but he was now pairing socks, and it was sweet that he was pairing mine as well as his own, not just leaving mine in a heap. He was actually stuffing one sock of each pair inside the other, and doing this with mine as well as his own. Spinning things out, knowing that it was silly to go off and get himself killed for no good effect?

'Neil, this country is under attack and you're raking up things from twenty years ago.'

He sounded unhappy, not contemptuous. I took pity on him. I didn't say that the principle was the same, his making crucial decisions like he was a single man, no other half to consider and consult. So I switched tacks, though I knew I didn't have a very strong segue.

'You said "this country". Fighting for your *country*. Funny, I'd never thought of you as the type.' I spoke as though we were having a conversation that had no bearing on anything that was about to happen. '"Ask not what your country can do for you – ask what you can do for your country." "I regret that I have only one life to lose for my country." "It is dulci et decorum, something like that, to die for one's country." Gosh, so that's you, and I never knew in thirty-two years.'

He'd finished sorting the socks and was now looking about him in a slightly distracted way, as if not knowing what to do next. I was getting through to him. I went on, 'Countries are artificial things, aren't they? Not really things to die for. They're what they are because of historical accidents, usually involving thugs and brutes, otherwise known as kings and barons and earls. Accidents like: some king's horses couldn't charge in 1497 or whenever because the ground was too muddy.'

'It's just a way of talking about things that are important. Freedom. Justice. Peace.' He banged a cupboard shut – the cupboard where he keeps his blood pressure medication, losartan and lercanidipine. No, it wasn't anger; or if it was, it was anger that I was getting through to him.

'And the people you care for?'

'Of course.' He muttered it. A reluctant return to sense?

'Okay,' he said, and that was the last thing I heard him say. The tone of voice was ambiguous, not quite brisk and businesslike, not quite a defeated sigh. So what he said could be taken in two different ways. Way number 1: he's completed all he needs to put together, he just needs the rucksack to stack his stuff in it, and then he'll make his forever farewell to me before walking out the door. Way number 2: he's come back to himself, he realises the truth of all I've been driving at, he's abandoning his death-wish (because that's what it is), he's about to acknowledge I'm right and is about to embrace me, the piles of socks and underwear and shirts and sweaters still stacked on the bed but totally irrelevant. Perhaps we'd just push them off and lie motionless together in their place on the rich heavy maroon counterpane, our embrace the whole world.

I realised I didn't want to know which of these possibilities he intended his 'Okay' to express. Quickly, I said, 'Your rucksack,' and exited the bedroom.

In the basement, things seemed to be resting quietly, away from an unsympathetic world. I remember there was a cold, slightly metallic smell, and that I wondered whether it could be the smell of dry rot – the flat owners had had to have dry rot treatment in the roof. I soon found the rucksack. It was on one of his mother's garden chairs, on top of some packets of rice I'd stockpiled that were now beyond their use-by date. He'd acquired the rucksack as a teenager for a school trip walking in the Salzkammergut, and in the album I put together a long time ago of photos of each of us before we met, there were ones of him on the trip, the colour somewhat bleached out, Drummond staring rather moodily at the camera as if there were lacks in his life that, without realising it, he was waiting for me to fill. I could hurry back upstairs with the rucksack and a supportive smile - see, I'm a nice guy, attentive to your wishes - and that might - just might - tip the balance, making him unwilling to abandon someone so ready and willing to take on his concerns. On the other hand, he might thank me, stuff his things into the rucksack, go into the en suite loo for a last pee, maybe with the rucksack already on his back, maybe saying with the door open that there was no other decision he could make, and that would be my last memory of him.

It flashed on me upon me that perhaps he'd joined up without telling me because he knows I'm too cowardly and selfish to do a thing like that so wanted to save me from feeling under pressure to go along and join up with him, and again I knew why I loved him.

I inspected the straps and canvas, looking for rot or decay that might make the rucksack unusable. I attempted a few rips with an old rusty hand fork to enhance its unusability. But perhaps, I thought, I should just tell him I couldn't find it. In the corner of the basement room used by the Hendersons, who lived in the flat below ours, there was an untidy heap of old carpet, and I stuffed the rucksack into it, out of sight. And then I just mooched around the basement, delaying for as long as possible going back up to Drummond, pleased that there was no sound of him coming down to look for it himself. I imagined his footsteps thumping on the stairs and then him saying in an accusing voice, 'I thought you knew where it was.' Because I hadn't hurried back up to our flat with it, enabling him to dash off to war a good many minutes before, I killed him. I think I did hear the blast. Or maybe it was the sound of another missile, different from the one that hit our house. There wasn't much left of the house above the basement, and the two Henderson children and their mother also died. I was in the one corner of the basement that wasn't totally buried in rubble from above.

Somehow, the fact that there was not much body for a funeral made easier to decide what Drummond meant by that last 'Okay'.

As I've said, I honestly think the things he said didn't express any contempt for me for not joining up like he did. Doesn't that mean he wasn't as sure of his decision as he pretended? If he was sure of his decision, wouldn't he have tried to persuade me to join him? Which he didn't. Of course, you could say that that was just an aspect of him being, as I'd pointed out to him, so atomic. You could try to see it just as respecting other people and their choices. He showed that as regards children. He'd wanted to adopt. 'We can give something to deprived kids,' he said when I found him watching a programme about adoption on TV. I noted the plural and also that the private pleasure he'd take in parenthood was being disguised behind an altruistic front. I made it clear I wasn't enthusiastic. I said that as gay men growing up under Section 28 that clamped down on the so-called 'promotion' of homosexuality, we'd had a struggle to make sense of ourselves and our lives and to find each other, and now we deserved to be able to enjoy being together without the hassles and distractions of parenthood. 'Okay,' he said, and left it there, and never came back to it again. No attempt to persuade me, no suggestion that, contrary to being a distraction, kids would bring us more fully together. I suppose if we had adopted, he might have thought twice about going off to shoot at an invading army. I can even feel a bit jealous of the children we never adopted.

But there's something else there, in this not trying to persuade me to join up, not criticising me for not signing up with him. It's not, it wasn't, just respect for other people's choices. If you really think that foreign troops landing requires an ordinary guy like you to sign up for the military, even though you're getting on in years and will be part of a sort of barely trained gang of amateurs, can you really avoid thinking that all the rest ought to do the same and that anyone who doesn't is a contemptible shirker? Unless, maybe, they're a key worker like a firefighter or a surgeon. If he really thought it was his duty to join up like he did - well, he wasn't superman, he was nobody out of the ordinary (except to me), so it must be anyone's duty. Including mine. So the fact that he never suggested I was a shirker, made no attempt to persuade me to join him, meant he must have had doubts about what he'd done. So when he said 'Okay', the last thing he ever said, he was going to agree with me and not leave me to go off to war.

RIVER

THE RIVER IS made of

many layers, staining and shining. Its depths soft, silky palimpsests fractured by molecules that spin and drift. You cannot read the edges. It holds its dazzle like a shield.

I lie on my stomach, right there in the soaking reeds. Early summer, grass fat with sap, birds singing horribly. The sun so bold my skin shrinks from its touch.

I close my eyes.

Still my head swarms with sensation, its cavities a red veined throb.

Better in the house, yet he was there.

I'll go for a walk I said. *Get fresh air.*

Good idea! We should!

The hope in his voice. He tried to hide the extent of it, the desperate extent.

Each wave announced by heat and pain behind the eyes, by colours sharp and tearing. So it begins. Cobweb on the light flex, wags like a finger, fine frail shadows. Too late to stop. The ceiling dips and curves, an eerie jig, its white silence blotted by hands grasping, voices rasping. Walls ripple and bulge, a breeze shivers the apartment through locked windows.

I'll go for a walk.
Get some.
Fresh.
air.

The soil is soft where the river has sucked. Even so it aches against my hipbones. I eat what he puts in front of me. I don't care, a corner of cold toast, soup from a spoon. But everything tastes of metal.

Leaving the house so fresh I gasp and grit my plastic teeth against the sky's new spinning. High and full of tiny clouds, as if the blue of it has curdled. Mackerel sky. Flesh and oil. The garden stinks of privet, the hedge robust to the point I can almost hear its tiny leaves squeaking. The ash tree on the corner, branches cleft like the hooves of the devil, shake like raven wings. Black white sharp knife. I have to get through. Stumbling onwards, car in the lane, blaring its horn yes fuck you too. Over the stile and down the footpath, rushing to a place forever cool and hidden.

I close my eyes.
Fresh air.
I'll come with you.
No. No.

It hurts to look at him. So clean. So goddam young and clean.

I unclench my fists to fill my palms with grass again. Mud thickens my nails. I plant myself. Hold on.

I could live on a boat. People do. In a van. Under a hedge. All I need is a lair. A tiny flat would do, on an estate where people like him don't dare to go, in their check shirts and bouji aftershave. Where you can sleep in your clothes if you prefer, and never bother to be cheerful.

Here is the river, running past like time itself. A river like this is best for children, nimble, high-pitched with enthusiasm. It's too fast for me.

Once there was time.

And then there was

none.

Fresh. Air.

I'll come with you. It's better.

I didn't fight. I slid the dress he handed me over my arms, laced up my sandals. Once I'd have loved to look like this. Clean, cossetted. Expensive.

I'll get my keys, he said. *Won't be a tick.*

I didn't know how long he planned to be. Before he was back I'd grasped the catch of the front door, not locked thank God, not yet. And I was out in the fresh wet air, as fast as I could in my stupid shoes.

On the river's wrinkling skin, tiny things are dancing. Midges, the size of atoms, skater beetles tracing figures of eight. I stare into the water, deciphering the face that trembles below them. An eyebrow and cheekbone, a nose and chin, coming and going like some stupid jigsaw. Who is the woman who floats there in pieces?

I used to think I knew.

How long ago was that?

Long, long ago.

I look deep, past my own face. As the green ribbons of the river flicker and untie I recognise with surprise a street down there, a hard city street. Pinprick shine from shop windows. Pavements that change colour with the lights – red, amber, green. It's all there, the corner shop, the DIY store, the glow of the bookies, the one before the nail bar. And I'm moving along it, as freely as I did when I was twenty, spaghetti straps and sunburn, gladiator sandals bought in the sale. I can hear the city sounds now, crack shot of heels, drum n bass of car stereos intersecting with summer folk songs. I taste spearmint, smell diesel. There's the ice cream shop on the corner, so many flavours, expensive, candy pink, went out of business years ago but here it is and here I am running for the tube, down the silver escalators, swept faster and faster by the current of time.

It's dark in the underground. Darkness roars past like a train. My head is full of it.

A phone rings far away.

It startles me.

It rings.

I can't shake it off.

I do not want to answer.

I like it here.

I do not in hell want to answer.

But it rings, like a rush of bubbles.

And rings, a sore gulp air.

For a walk. That's all. Yeah.

Fresh air. You know?

Once the river was moving.

Now it's still.

The river is made of

marble.

ALISON MOORE

WHERE ARE THEY NOW?

THE GIRL ARRIVED just as Miss Haimes was scraping up the last smears of her sticky cake. Setting down her fork, Miss Haimes gestured for the girl to take a seat at her table. 'Please,' she said. The girl settled herself on the red banquette, dumping a huge shoulder bag between them. Miss Haimes dabbed at her mouth with her paper serviette and said, 'You're late.'

'I didn't recognise you,' said the girl, as if that were her reason, as if she had been looking and looking for her, whereas Miss Haimes had seen her, through the window, dallying with a boy in a car before coming into the café at two minutes past. 'You look nothing like your photos,' added the girl, taking in, supposed Miss Haimes, the way her face had fallen, the wrinkles that her make-up could not hide, the roots coming through beneath the dye. The girl rifled through the contents of her enormous bag.

'Can you find anything in there?' asked Miss Haimes. She knew exactly what she had in her own little handbag: her purse and her keys and her tissues and that was it. She would be lost with a cavernous bag like that.

The girl smiled and brought out a piece of paper and a recording device which she set on the table between them.

'You don't mind?' she asked, pressing the little red button. 'So, this is just a kind of fun little magazine article, a "Where Are They Now?" piece. You know, when someone used to be famous and you wonder what happened to them?'

'Yes,' said Miss Haimes.

The girl consulted her notes, which were written in green biro on her single scrap of paper. Her handwriting was careless, and illegible to Miss Haimes. 'So, you were an actress?'

'Yes, I am an actress,' said Miss Haimes. She spoke rather sharply and a wet crumb of cake flew from her mouth and landed on the table between them.

'You were in *loads* of films. I've seen some clips on YouTube.' The girl read out the titles she had scribbled down.

'They weren't my best,' said Miss Haimes. She named some films that had been more positively received, but the girl had not heard of them. Miss Haimes mentioned her final film, which had been something of a flop but she expected that the name of her co-star would impress the girl.

The girl looked blank. 'Richard who?' she said. 'How's that spelt?'

A waitress arrived at their table, and the girl ordered a salad. Miss Haimes slid her gaze over the cake display and ordered a scone with jam and cream. There was still some tea in her pot and she poured it out.

'And then . . .' said the girl.

'And then what?' asked Miss Haimes, stirring sugar into her tea.

'People will be wondering where you've gone.'

'I've not gone anywhere,' said Miss Haimes. 'I'm right here, where I've always been.'

'But what have you been doing,' asked the girl, 'in between then and now?'

The waitress returned with their order, and Miss Haimes set about spreading her scone. The girl's salad was heavy with red onion, the health benefits of which were legendary – it was good for indigestion and insomnia and arthritic pain and so many other things – but it gave Miss Haimes heartburn. For the remainder of their conversation she would be able to smell it on the girl's breath.

The door to the street opened, and a noisy, laughing group came in with the cold. 'I was offered panto,' said Miss Haimes. They used to come in here after rehearsals. And in all that time, she thought, looking around at the décor, nothing seemed to have changed. Perhaps the red banquettes had been reupholstered; she didn't remember them looking so cheap.

The girl, gesturing to the recording device and the noisy group that was now moving away, said, 'Would you repeat that?'

Miss Haimes took a sip of her sugary tea and shook her head.

The girl had expressed an interest in coming to her home, but Miss Haimes was glad to have kept her away. She closed the door to her apartment and slipped off her shoes. They were her smartest pair, but they hurt her heels. She put them back on the rack and walked in stockinged feet along the hallway to her living room. She expected the girl would have admired her wallpaper with its vibrant birds, and her many antique mirrors. She imagined the girl eyeing and touching her things, searching her framed photographs, asking questions, wanting to open closed doors.

There was not a single room in this apartment in which Miss Haimes could not hear her neighbours. Through her walls, she heard their lovemaking, their singing in the shower, their children crying. Her ceiling shook with the pounding feet of the people who lived overhead.

No, she thought - walking over to her CD player, her old bone china rattling inside her glass-fronted cabinet - she could not have borne the girl's presence in her apartment, the inspection of her life. Pressing 'play' on the disc that was already in the drive, she wondered if the girl liked John Barry.

She did regret agreeing to meet the girl in the café though. It sold the most wonderful cakes and pastries, but she had been avoiding the place. She had been good, drinking nothing but warm water and cleansing smoothies to which she added herbs she grew herself. It was a regime to benefit the body and the soul.

But the moment she had entered the café, she had slipped back into her old habits. She had wanted that gluey cake, that rich scone, that sweet tea, but she should not have had them. She could still taste them.

'I'll call you,' the girl had said, lifting that big, bright bag of hers onto her shoulder, 'if there's anything else.'

Ever since then, Miss Haimes had been expecting her to ring. Occasionally, passing the phone that sat on a spindly table in her hallway, she lifted the handset to hear the dialling tone; she checked that the handset was sitting correctly in its cradle and that the phone line was secure in its socket. It made her feel like a lovesick teenager, waiting for a call from some boy, who had already got what he wanted from her and would not, after all, be calling.

She had an extension by her bed. She used to have the most beautiful bed, in the most beautiful house, when she lived with her mother. As a child, Miss Haimes had adored her mother, who had been rather aloof. In late adulthood, it had occurred to Miss Haimes that her mother did not love her. This was towards the end of her mother's life. She still missed that house and tried not to think of it.

There had been a garden too, in which she had grown vegetables as well as herbs. She had done all the cooking. She had kept a flower garden too, although some of the herbs were just as pretty: the dill had jolly clusters of yellow flowers, and the rosemary had lovely pale purple blooms, and the monkshood had gorgeous deep purple flowers – you just had to remember that they were toxic. She no longer had a garden, but she still had her herbs which she kept in little pots.

She had had to get rid of so much when she moved into this poky little apartment: she had given up most of the furniture, as well as antiques and paintings. The bed she had now was rather narrow and decidedly ugly. She sat down on the edge of the mattress, lifted the extension onto her lap and dialled the girl's number.

'I didn't finish telling you about Richard,' she said.

'Richard?' said the girl.

'I had a lot of admirers,' said Miss Haimes. 'But Richard and I were in love.' By the time they filmed their final scenes, things between them had soured, but she did not tell the girl that. She hadn't asked a lot of him, but sometimes she just needed to hear his voice, to know he was there at the end of the line. She called when the night was just too long, though it angered him, and his wife.

The girl sounded as if she were outside, in a public place,

perhaps in a park. Miss Haimes pictured her pushing a child on a swing.

'Do you have children?' asked Miss Haimes.

'I'm only eighteen,' said the girl. She was even younger than Miss Haimes had imagined. She seemed so confident, whereas Miss Haimes, at that age, had felt lost.

'You can have a child at eighteen,' said Miss Haimes.

There was a pause. Miss Haimes could hear the wind, and people in the background.

'You don't have children, do you?' asked the girl, as Miss Haimes returned her handset to its cradle.

After the film with Richard, work had rather dried up. At the time, she was still living with her mother in that beautiful old house. She could keep herself busy with her hobbies, her gardening, her baking, but the months went by and the phone didn't ring and she feared it might never ring again.

Richard had eventually moved away with his family, going ex-directory while he was at it. She found him anyway. It wasn't difficult – he was still appearing on stage, still a public figure.

He had always liked her jam tarts, so she baked a batch especially for him, 'as a peace offering,' she said to his son as she handed them over. It wasn't possible, of course, for her to go to his house – Richard would have refused to see her, and his wife would have called the police – so she had intercepted his son on his way home from school. 'Just for your daddy,' she told him. 'He'll know who they're from.'

She had been drinking at the time; she had been drinking too much for months – pickling herself, said her mother. When she got really bad, she had to go cold turkey. After the jam tarts, she gave up baking; she gave up sugar and alcohol, what her mother called her nasty habits, her little addictions. She took herself out for daily walks, which her mother referred to as 'walking the streets'. She was trying to be good, and she was for a while, but then she was offered the panto, which both her agent and her accountant advised her to do, and her diet went to hell.

'Are you back again?' asked the waitress.

Miss Haimes ignored the question and ordered a piece of caramel cake. From her window seat, waiting for her cake to arrive, she watched the world going by. The theatre over the road was all lit up.

She had played the Wicked Queen, a role her mother had said suited her down to the ground. 'Take that look off your face,' she had added, 'I'm joking.'

The rest of the cast were rather young, and Miss Haimes had expected to find herself somewhat outside their circle, but after the first rehearsal, the girls had linked their arms through hers as they crossed the road to the café. She had never felt so included.

There was a striking young man called Benjamin, who was playing Muddles. He was not *young*, she supposed, but he was younger than she was. His costume was ridiculous, but he had tremendous stage presence. He was charming off stage as well and paid great attention to Miss Haimes in the green room. He looked at her with his big, brown eyes and said he was a fan of her work. She told him he could not have been old enough to see her films when they came out.

'Yeah,' he said, 'but you can find clips of all these old films on YouTube.'

She told him he ought to be chasing after girls his own age, but she agreed to drinks.

He took her to a little pub she didn't know and paid for her gin and tonic. She looked great, he said, in those YouTube clips. She discovered he was familiar with the film she had done with Richard. 'I know it was bad,' he said, 'but it was kind of *good* bad?'

Some of the reviews had been brutal, although her mother had said, 'I don't think it's your *worst* film.'

'You looked great anyway,' said Benjamin. He searched on his phone for a clip, wanting to show her, as if she had never seen herself before. He turned the screen towards her, and there was Richard, talking to her, touching her, the two of them trapped in time together. He had loved her then, or had said he did.

Benjamin, putting his phone away, said, 'You still look great for your age.' In between gulps of beer, he quoted some of Richard's lines in a way Miss Haimes disliked, as if it had been a comedy.

Richard was a serious actor. He would not be caught dead in a pantomime. He had done Shakespeare. Miss Haimes had longed to do Shakespeare but she had never been offered a part. Richard had played princes and kings.

Miss Haimes was finishing her third double gin when Benjamin said, 'Enough about this Richard. I think we'd better get you home.'

She let him come inside, knowing her mother was already in bed, fast asleep after her Horlicks, with a sleeping pill crushed up and stirred in for good measure. 'Let's have a nightcap,' said Miss Haimes. 'Let's make ourselves comfortable.' She wished Richard could see her; she wanted to call him, to tell him she had another man now, a younger man.

It became a semi-regular thing: a few drinks at this secluded pub and then back to her house. She told her mother she had a boyfriend, expecting her to be pleased. 'At your age?' said her mother. 'Don't make a fool of yourself.'

The caramel cake arrived, and Miss Haimes turned away from the window. The first forkful made her jaw ache – it was terribly sweet – but she ate it all.

After films, the theatre had been a shock – having to say the same lines and wear the same costume and lurid stage make-up day after day, week in, week out. It was hard to imagine it ever coming to an end.

About halfway through the run – backstage before a performance, through a sticky mist of hairspray – she heard that Benjamin was seeing a make-up girl. The other girls were laughing, saying he'd tried it on with everyone, apparently even with . . . But then one of the girls had turned and seen Miss Haimes, and no more had been said.

The panto ran for months, right through the winter, and it was ghastly: those relentless appearances, the grotesquery, the laughter, the interminable critics. Miss Haimes had stopped going to the café, and she had stopped going to the pub. She no longer spoke to the others off stage, with the exception of the phone calls, which she never remembered making but sometimes she woke in her beautiful bed with the receiver on her pillow, and an empty bottle of something cheap on her nightstand, and then there'd be the backstage looks and comments and those tiresome warnings, and she'd have to hide the phone bill from her mother.

⚜

'I haven't told you about my childhood,' said Miss Haimes. She was calling from the phone in the hallway of her apartment and wished she had a stool to sit on, or that she had called from the bedroom. She was feeling a little bit weak in the legs.

After a moment, the girl said, 'Well, what did you want me to know?'

'It was nice,' said Miss Haimes. 'It was a nice childhood.'

'All right,' said the girl. Miss Haimes wondered if she was writing this down.

'As a teenager, I had a lot of admirers.'

The girl made a non-committal noise.

'If you like,' said Miss Haimes, 'you can come to my apartment. We can talk some more.' She did think the girl would like the colourful birds on her wallpaper.

'No, it's fine,' said the girl. 'Thanks though.'

'I expect I could spare an hour or so.'

'There's no need,' said the girl. 'I've finished the article.'

'Already?' said Miss Haimes. 'That was quick.'

There were actually only four birds in the design, all game birds, arranged in an endlessly repeating pattern.

'They'll probably want a photograph,' said Miss Haimes. 'When is it going to be published?'

'I don't know,' said the girl. 'I'll call you.'

'All right,' said Miss Haimes.

The girl hung up first. Miss Haimes went to the kitchen to pulverise some vegetables, and then went to the café. She asked for hot chocolate and said yes when they offered her cream and marshmallows on top, and she found it so sickly she could barely finish it.

When the panto season finally drew to a close, she had found herself, once again, at a loose end. Her mother said she ought to consider secretarial work, seeing as that was what she was qualified for. 'Although,' she added, 'they might not want you now. That world's moved on without you. You'd be lost in a modern office.'

Miss Haimes had gone walking, just to get out of the house. She found herself walking out to where Benjamin lived. She stood outside his building, a brutalist monstrosity, only knowing that he might be in there somewhere. She had not stopped thinking about him and was overcome by a determination to see him. She knew he worked, in between acting jobs, in a local pub, so tracking him down was quite easy.

He was in the middle of pulling a pint, and looked surprised to see her, but she had every right to sit at the bar. She ordered a drink. 'And one for yourself,' she added.

She told him she'd missed him. He took a long look at her. 'You look good,' he said. She had made a special effort.

She stayed seated at the bar. In between serving customers, Benjamin drifted over and stood talking to her. It seemed his relationship with the make-up girl had ended badly. 'Young women can be very demanding,' said Miss Haimes. She ordered another drink, 'and one for yourself.'

At closing time, he agreed to walk her home. On the doorstep, he agreed to come in for a nightcap.

'For old times' sake,' he said.

She fixed him a drink. She knew what he liked. 'I bet you're hungry as well, aren't you?' she said, going into the kitchen.

She didn't have to worry about disturbing her mother, who was out for the count.

It had come as a shock when, after her mother's death, Miss Haimes had been obliged to sell the beautiful house, along with the garden in which she had done so much work, and move into this cheap apartment.

Once again, she had sworn off drinking and all her bad habits, determined to make a fresh start. She committed to her diet of warm water and homemade smoothies, and she went walking, though she tried not to pass the beautiful house in which she used to live. When, on occasion, she found herself standing outside it, she saw that very little had changed, and thought that it would not seem strange to fetch a key from her handbag and let herself in. But she knew, in reality, she was likely to find that her key no longer worked. She envied the family living there now.

She tried very hard not to dwell on the past, on Richard and his family, on Benjamin with his puppy-dog eyes, on her mother. She kept her apartment clean and tended to her herbs and took her walks and the years went quietly by.

Then the girl had got in touch, requesting this interview for what she called a profile piece in a glossy magazine. Miss Haimes had been reluctant at first. She did not want to be put through the wringer. She did not want to open a can of worms. But the girl had seemed so keen, so interested, that in the end Miss Haimes agreed. The girl had suggested meeting in the café opposite the theatre. 'It's close to you, I think,' she said, 'so that would be convenient?'

Was that a statement, thought Miss Haimes, or a question? She said, 'That will be fine.'

'What time is it?' asked the girl. Her tired sigh sounded so much like one of Richard's that Miss Haimes laughed.

'Did I wake you?' she said. She steadied herself against the spindly telephone table and focused on her wallpaper, on the garish birds, the fat pheasants waiting to be shot. All her lights were on, and someone had been banging on the wall. She didn't know what time it was; it was hard to keep track. She had no clock in her hallway, and though she peered at her watch, she could not read its blurry face.

'Are you still there?' asked the girl.

Miss Haimes said she was. As if to prove it, she turned to catch her reflection in one of her heavy and elaborate mirrors. She hardly recognised herself.

'Are you all right?' asked the girl.

'Quite all right,' said Miss Haimes. 'Did I tell you about my childhood?'

'Yes,' said the girl.

'I'm happy to talk more,' said Miss Haimes. 'I could come to you.'

'There's no need,' said the girl.

'But I could.'

Now, she thought, she had lowered herself in the girl's eyes.

'I expect the magazine will want a photograph,' said Miss Haimes. 'They usually do.'

She could hear the rustle of bedding. She heard a man's voice, a complaint.

'I'm returning to the theatre,' said Miss Haimes. 'I'm being considered for a number of roles. It seems I'm in demand.'

The girl had gone. Miss Haimes replaced the receiver.

ఇ

She was sick, now, again, of her overindulgence. Her mother had frequently reproached her for her intemperance, her lack of control, though Miss Haimes knew that she was capable of a great deal of control.

There were some empty bottles on her nightstand. She carried them into the kitchen, rinsed them out and put them aside for recycling. Her face, reflected in the window behind the sink, with the night behind it, looked shocking. It was like being watched by a stranger who was standing outside in the cold, and when she turned away she could imagine that the stranger was still there, watching her.

She had no appetite, but she prepared a smoothie just as if she were making it for somebody else, for a patient who needed to be taken care of. She hulled the strawberries, juiced the oranges, chopped the pineapple, taking pleasure in the sweet, sharp smells, the vivid colours. The herbs were looking healthy on the windowsill behind the chopping board; the dark purple flowers were so attractive.

She had a rainbow of colours in her blender, or the best part of a rainbow, all the warm colours: red, orange, yellow, purple, although perhaps purple was not truly warm, perhaps it was in between, or perhaps it was cold. Normally, she would add avocado, or spinach – which would turn the whole thing green and make it look like a witch's brew – but she wanted all the sweetness. And she wanted sleep. She had the last of her mother's sleeping pills. The nightgown into which she changed was one she had kept from the set of her film with Richard. She wondered if the girl would have been interested in that.

Miss Haimes slipped under the covers. Her bedroom door was ajar and the light was on in the hallway, though it was years since she'd been afraid of the dark, or of being alone in it. She could see the bright, beady-eyed birds.

Miss Haimes left the stage. The backstage lighting was dreadful, but she pressed on along the corridor. She started to say, 'Is this right?' but she was alone. She was wondering if she'd come off the wrong way, if she ought to go back. She could still hear applause in the auditorium; she could hear cheering and whistling. She ought to have waited, to have done another curtain call.

The corridor seemed impossibly long. She'd been walking and walking. She wanted her dressing room. She wanted to take off this heavy costume, this uncomfortable corset, this itchy wig. She wanted to get this thick make-up off her face.

The noise from the audience had finally died down, or else she was too far away to hear it. She walked on. There was old scenery leaning against the walls: two-dimensional forests and cities and palaces. There were props, just left there in the corridor, and she had to go carefully between and around them. It was inconvenient, not to mention hazardous. And it was so dark: unable to see far ahead, she kept expecting the corridor to end, but it just kept on going. She could still turn back, but she didn't want to look foolish.

She had not seen a single door in these bare walls. She was trying to remember what her dressing room even looked like, if she would recognise it when she came to it, *if* she ever came to it. It did not really seem possible for this endless corridor to still be within the theatre.

She was just on the brink of giving in and turning around,

facing that long walk back to an empty stage, when she came to the end of the corridor, and there in front of her was a door that was surely the door to her dressing room, though perhaps it was just a cleaning cupboard, or perhaps she would discover an office, or perhaps it just led to the street.

It was cold in that corridor; she was freezing, despite the weight of her costume and her long walk from the stage, and she hoped that her dressing room would be warm.

As soon as she opened the door, she saw she was not alone. As the leading lady, she would have expected to have her own dressing room. Or perhaps this was the green room, a common room. It was somehow hard to tell what sort of room it was, it was so bare, and of indeterminate size, and it was not warm after all. It might have been a backstage storeroom. It took her a moment to recognise the little boy standing before her, but of course it was Richard's son; he had Richard's eyes. And there was Benjamin, who did not look so charming now. 'Come in, come in,' said her mother. She was wearing one of her thin nighties, and Miss Haimes said, 'Aren't you cold?'

She sensed others too, but when she tried to look she saw the boy again, in his little school uniform, and Benjamin, with his tremendous presence, and her mother, saying *Take that look off your face*. Miss Haimes turned away, but there they were: the boy, his face and fingers sticky with jam, and Benjamin, saying *You don't look so great*, and her mother, who looked disapproving and most unkind. Miss Haimes wanted someone to loosen her corset; she wanted water; she wanted them not to be staring like this, like the beady-eyed birds on the wallpaper, repeating endlessly.

INSIDE

HAD A HUSBAND once, for a year and a day, but no child, although I pretend I do have one, a boy, now and then. Craig, my craggy Craig about eight then again ten depending on who I'm with – must keep track – anyway always a little boy to tell them about, neighbours and pals, a boy I play football with on the beach, though there's no beach. I'm quite good at football, I know the names of footballers, watch it now and then – cup finals and things – and the boy would have a 'mop of hair' I would ruffle and comb and remark on in the mornings when we had our breakfast and I asked him about schoolwork. Now of course home-school work, downloading lessons and whatnot.

The gone husband? Practised the niceties, touch of religion in him like a slim line running through his body ending in the little tail peeping out. Like Harry after him he picked me up at work, or I him, I forget, but unlike H went through all the hoo-ha of a divorce to marry me. But I think he missed the guilt, the delicious guilt, for him a would-be man of the cloth. Yes, a wannabe vicar. Flirted with it, he said (flirted with everything, I said), felt a calling in my youth and applied to *theological* college. He liked that word. How could he be a vicar, his hands all over women and the world, what little of it he got offered, his fingerprints of grease and want, his speech fouling up perfectly good air. It's a twisty, cunting road you put us on, oh Lord, you deal out your hands unevenly: him in his wanky prayers every night.

His guilt like pillows and clouds reclined on, but he also ranted and stamped his foot. He thought he was endearing and lovable, his mother encouraging him, standing by his side on visits and simpering.

He was a box ticker, out walking he'd see an old fort, the ruins of a monastery with always the joke about my face, nod at it, tick it off mentally, and walk on. 'Got the T-shirt' a favourite phrase of his, along with 'to be fair' - he had a strange idea of fair. Womanising was fair, in that it was *natural*.

He got rid of the microwave, heard it gave you cancer but continued to smoke until recently - I hear now he vapes. I was a box ticked off, took little more than a year to get to the bottom of me. Now I am a divorcee, I am a spinster like my aunt was. She would be on at me about my slovenliness, my manners, the way I'm bringing up Craig. She appears in my dreams now, brushing my hair obsessively, until it gleams and more, until my eyes fall out.

He could be kicky, he would leave you in a service station in a faraway town built in the 80s or in a coronavirus hotspot on a Sunday if there had been coronavirus around in those days; he could be tie wearing and corduroy and desert boot, kind looking, wispy but behind closed doors in his car on the corner of roads or in the back of some out of town Cotswold stone bar, some midday bar he could be sharp, grip you, the hissing tongue of him slipping around. That sharpness that pout and the silence in the mornings was just like my mother's ex before he died, before they both died: do we marry a type?

Wonder what he'll be up to now seeking out some vicarry truth with his new woman or practising some bon mot some one liner to give out to the neighbour tomorrow as he wishes them good day the breath of him rancid.

Two or so years after hubby was Harry and he worked right up the corridor and took his turn in my queue at lunchtime. I was always Harry's as soon as he arrived and trained us in things we already knew.

Just before lockdown the girls got together for a reunion and never told me, back in the area and making myself known. That was a mistake because I'm going to gatecrash the next one and go round and remind them of their misdemeanours loudly in the chosen pub, packets of crisps ripped open to be shared on the tables, rolls and sausage rolls and rolls of sound about the past and what it was like for them which teacher lost control who set fire to their hair in Chemistry who wrote what on the board, the class bully the class victims still in the seating arrangements. Evelyn the organiser (I learn from Facebook) has got bustier and reddened her hair in line with her husband and child. I met her somewhere on the school run I forget where and she told me not to call her Eve any more, nobody did any more.

School to me a long damp corridor, squatting grey and red brick buildings amongst sparse trees; dark headed bald headed bewigged teachers spouting, the road to revolution, the inner logic of atoms. Three blind mice. Disintegration of interest was rapid, felt it crumble crumble inside.

A dinner maybe a dance do they still have dinner and dances? Do they still play darts? The football machine we all played do you remember that in the sixth form, the games of bridge, never played it since I will say. Oh I have, Evelyn, bosomy and nurturing, will say, I play it all the time and there are fortnightly schools round my house if you want to come, new packs each time, bring a nice bottle of wine. That's how it would go, and I would get in with that crowd, the bridge playing, sports car brigade and maybe for some weeks they'd let me in, and speak of their gardens and lovers and spa days, while they swapped cards about in their hands, the days ahead, the days forgotten, but one day one night with drink consumed, the Labrador on the rug behind us in the room with spotlit framed prints of holiday views on the walls, they'd say I ruined it with my questions and peculiar smell.

There were men before and between husband number one - I'm optimistic - who I called Oswald though his name was Neville, and Harry, my dark-haired Harry who was, is, with his even features and clear eyes his voice like something humming, a cleaned-up version of Oswald, my husband put through the wash, a bolder smoother version, one with all his worries and twitches ironed out.

Other men went by and by. The best of them out of reach, frying their own fish, their own books to read, programmes to watch, hobbies to maintain and laughs to laugh with someone else. The one with McCartney's accent but who couldn't sing. The one who always talked of our 'love' when there wasn't any, little. The hairs in this one's nose and ears, his views on the Arab spring and his skunky genitals and Premiership football obsession: he moved in for a while, measured our weeks by matches and then left at the end of the season.

Cold cold ones who wanted stuff from you, sex, a play made from it, a particular two scene act over and over again and got you to dress like this or like that maybe it's their mother fantasies or a girl seen when they were adolescent forming ideas about who women were, what they were like. One told me men – all? – are after reliving a moment over and over and fixated a lot of them on first loves or aunties or cousins seen first in the nude or half nude at someone's paddling pool party with younger kids about giving it a soundtrack of wellbeing, pretend screams and hide and seek and splashes, water droplets on skin, sunlight. I never had that, siblings, afternoons splashing in the garden.

Imagine if I'd stayed with this or that 'boyfriend'. Stalk them on Facebook with their wives their trips to the zoo and getting the sled out in winter. Men on a merry-go-round in my head, the dropping-off points. Harry never online and now we're all working from home I never see him except in glimpses when I drive to his street and park opposite to watch him and his wife walk by and take in her size and gait next to him, see how they fit together, the places they touch, elbow and hip, kids running behind and before making bombing noises, chuckling and singing, three mites: I know the order of them, gender, age, but not what they smell like. He never looks over to see my best side.

Imagine all the kids I could have had, not just one, how they would grow up I could tell them secrets I could lead them astray I could sing them a song I could follow them around I would go to their dens I would ruin their lives.

COVID did for us. I'd see him at work even after he'd made me delete his flirty titbit emails, stood over me, pretending to help sort out my software, hissing like a slow puncture at me. Bit macho, I said, as he got me to empty the trash folder too, when are you due? The end he kept saying, the end got it? No following around no pissing about no eye widening, no big welcome when I come in or that movement of your knee, don't think I haven't noticed. I'm losing patience losing the will to live losing my temper now get on with it don't ring me don't message me don't look at me. Fucker, should have spat in his soup so to speak, snapped off his cock and presented it to his wife, instead the usual crying in the back of his car round the corner from his family watching Disney+ or gaming or social messaging on their devices, our phones turned off, Sunday sex or something like, a pulling of this, a smudging of that, some squirming about. Unsatisfactory, but I would have put up with it. I'd see him in the corridor, in the canteen, remembering our assignations in smaller and smaller hotels increasingly out of town, making our way up badly carpeted stairs. He only came back to my house once, said he could feel my aunt watching us, wouldn't come again.

After sex we'd sprawl together and discuss books. Well, I'd listen, his voice purring. Harry is a reader, the latest Booker winner, stuff like that. He said Marlon James was difficult, full of Jamaican patois, inside violent gangsters' heads, but it was worth it for the Bob Marley bits. (I sang 'Three Little Birds' in the shower once.) He got me reading novels again, all the way through, not the *Seven Killings*, but Austen, the Brontës, Hardy, stuff I read at school. With our love of different eras and genres we complemented each other. I said this to him, I said we'd make an ideal couple, and he agreed. He agreed.

He was going to run away with me to Mexico to France to Wales we were going to live up a mountainside with a view of the sea and catch rabbits or something or in a caravan by the side of a road or get jobs in a bar and be live-in staff in a little room with a sink and a black and white telly. Do they still have black and white tellies?

I told him I wouldn't mind if his kids visited, Christ they could even live with us (eventually). They could play in the back yard: I wouldn't trip them up. I would support, not like my aunt who never listened. I would cock my ear – I would be a proper mum, hug them, warn them of predators, introduce them to Craig. They would all get along. We'd be a chuckling family unit sweeping into restaurants and theme parks, joshing each other. People would look.

You know how sometimes people look wrongly put to-gether, their heads/faces not right for their bodies, their legs belong to someone else? Well, Harry fit together perfectly. He was all of a piece. He was a warm feeling like a drug that worked. Until he turned away, basically a coward with hair on his knuckles. Now with working from home I never see him going past my desk trying to avoid my eyes and me saying 'Hi Harry, how's the kids?' and him forced to look at me and saying fine. He even seems to avoid the zoom meetings we should be in together where maybe I could examine him, look for lines on that face, look for a wink in the little square he occupied but his head and shoulders never turn up.

Craig's growing up quickly going to secondary next term, now schools are re-opening, same one as I went to, St B's, naturally, he's not getting away with not being fucked up for life like the rest of us.

Indoors we play – the task of finding him over and over beneath curtains and round doors, he hid in a bin once I could have killed him the fright he gave me. We sing into broomsticks and hair dryers when I can get the little bugger off the sofa, he'll reluctantly sing Rihanna - 'Diamonds' - when I can unglue him from his World of Warcraft game. 'Screentime!' I admonish him, pointing to my non-existent watch. I'm a good mum, I protect him from bullies, I pursue his case down the school I wasn't letting the sourpuss Head have her way with my boy.

I scrimped and saved to bring him up properly, weaned him off his dad, Jesus botherer Oswald. Luckily he doesn't resemble him. We're settled now at my aunt's old house, a slab of terrace, with the wind pressing front and back. My aunt brought me up here from 8 onwards. Hardly noticing me, except to pinch and complain about my noise, preoccupied I thought, but what it was was Pick's disease setting in.

Harry moving on, or moving back to the skinny wife's arms. I was on the ball once, but deteriorating at a rate now, when I'm only 36 or 39 or 42.

Next door's music streaming, Alexa-ed into their rooms. Noisy bunch, now getting an extension until the pandemic stopped it. They used to have outdoors do's, laughter coming over with the smoke of barbecues, friends and family I presume standing on grass in heels with glasses of prosecco you swirl by the stem, nothing like that for them or anyone these days as we all sit in our houses unable to get out, *except for essentials.*

Everybody's in, all down the street, invisible crowds all about. Children, adults, dogs all stuffed next door both ways every hour of the day. Working from home like me - they can't do without me, without me information doesn't get distributed - or home schooling or lazing playing computer games like Craig always upstairs. In the evenings I watch Scandi-noir, it all looks so easy, hand-cuffed to a radiator.

I was going to be a new me, weren't we all once restrictions had been lifted and we could go running again. I had in mind long miles down the towpath and across parks only inadvertently showing up in his street again. I would join a running club. I bought all the gear, had it delivered but only tried it on once. Not my style. Leave that sort of thing to Evelyn or Harry's wife (Anna, Elaine – as if I didn't know). Instead I tried on dresses I hadn't put on since the divorce and I went on a few Tinder dates, black showing a little bosom when I leant over the steak and wine. They were all disappointing, Oswald-a-likes – is it me? Although with one suitably dark haired, stubbled, I stayed out all night by the canal drinking whisky out of a bottle. You're as fucked up as me, he said.

With the schools re-opened I bump into Evelyn and her cronies more and more on this corner or that, on their way to school or back.

Now for instance by the shops a group of them, assorted mates fresh from devouring each other's gossip last night when they played bridge and got mildly pissed. One with a dog, a blue grey greyhound thing on a lead, a pushchair or two. Empty trains go by over the bridge behind them. Evelyn says there should only be gatherings of six outside and I would make it seven. Only if you count the kids, I say. And I go round and look into the faces of these chewing, crying, uncaring toddlers, although one is smiling and it stops me, someone smiling at me. Lovely, lovely, they're all lovely, I say. I beam.

'Craig,' I say, straightening up, 'do you know the name stands for a mischievous and open person? I looked it up. "A

Craig is always athletic, hardworking and many ladies view him as handsome."'

I never let myself stink, I say to the group of mumble sharers who hate me, it's there in their pleated mouths and skirts, I take a shower at least three times a day. They lift their eyes to me temporarily to take in my cleanliness.

I offer my services, as humble as you like, I've read my Dickens, I say I'll pick up Adrian along with my Craig when he starts back, when he gets out of hospital because now he's gone and got the 'rona on top of all his usual problems. Complications. His lungs all sticky with it, like he's been smoking all his eleven years, I say, it was like someone else speaking. They stand the mandatory six feet away or so, black, blue, spotted, leopard skin masks tucked under their chins. Evelyn has a charity badge on her jumper. I think she's about to ask for money, sponsorship, but she is saying first time she let her Adrian walk home alone was heart stopping. She lightly thumps her breast.

'I let Craig do his own thing,' I tell her, 'room of his own to do whatever in. Don't go in there, just lean against the door now and then, strain to hear, but he's not noisy, you know, sadly, I'd like to hear some hip hop blasting out.'

'You can have mine for a night,' Evelyn laughs through her top front teeth. 'Do a swap.' Her Adrian she's offering me and I know he bullies Craig. Her Adrian who might become a banker like his dad, she'd said before on another corner, he's got that type of brain, bashed Craig nightly when he was about, when the time was ripe. Her son rangy and gloopy and not a patch on my compact kid even if hers is growing a scattered gingery moustache. Craig told me, back from school as *The Chase* was on when he should be doing his homework

learning about kings and queens and reading novels. 1984 and
Catch 22. He told me the ginger lad's reach was too long. He
told me gloomily how Adrian led a small gang determined to
humiliate him in lessons, it was Craig sir, craggy Craig, and
playtime, constantly coming up and sniping, pinching and
pulling and snapping little bits off my son, football star of
the future, the one who'll support me in old age, will maybe
watch me shrivel and burn like my aunt, who'll get me things
from the shop. They gouge out little bits of him and take
them away and throw them in drains and bramble until there
is nothing left.

"'I'm telling you honey,' I say to him,' I say to them ranged
across the shopfront pavement in their Ugg boots and mittens,
"'you've got to straighten up if you want to play for Villa.'"

So it was pick up the kid, the third, the easiest, with his flip-
floppy hair and his Harry eyes, snatch him from the street,
drive past and bundle him headfirst into the boot hurting
Harry where it hurts most, he told me he was his favourite, the
way he got lyrics wrong in songs, said diso-naur. Really show
him; could hide Junior in the basement, I'd go down and taunt
him about his blue eyes and his butter-and-stale-biscuit smell,
get him to sing a wrong lyrics song, except I haven't got a
basement, in the attic then the bathroom except workmen have
come back to populate the scaffolding next door. Workmen
drilling drilling at all levels, glimpses of work boots and calves
even though it's not sunny, shorts mandatory, tools stuffed
here and there they look as if they're about to enter through
the window. So no couldn't bring him here, even though I
could then parade him about down the shops, in front of
the gathering, ruffle his hair and say look here's Craig, not

exactly as described, younger, a fair bit younger, the famous Craig who can do 50 keepie-uppies can't you Craig, watched by Villa scouts on windy touchlines. Under my hand wholly, no thanks are due to his father, doesn't he look like me got my upturned nose and serene nature. When he's a footballer, a midfield dynamo, earning their and their husbands' annual salaries combined in a day, in an hour, the bridge players would let me in would be amazed at my progress how quickly I'd become an expert, trump them, I was always the one that was missing in their lives, the vaping lot of them, the piece that made them whole.

The disease took away many of my aunt's functions, speech, movement, digestion, and she had to go live in a nursing home. I took a train to visit now and then. Her eyes did lock on mine but otherwise nothing much. She used to hum along to songs, nursery rhymes, 'Grand Old Duke of York' but even that went. Instead I had one-sided conversations about her atrocious parenting skills and how ill equipped she'd left me. How we never went on holiday, and I used to watch the other families pack their cars and disappear in the summer and return burned and happy playing some new game they'd learned in the street. The elderly nurse would come to spoon-feed her sludge which she sometimes swallowed, talking to her and to me as if she understood. To get the food down the nurse had to massage her neck.

Her whole body thinned out, breastless, curled up, hands claws. Unmoving, clenched. I told her what she'd been like in those last few months at home, how she stood next to radiators until she burnt, how she gave all her money to toddlers in supermarkets and chased them down the aisles, as if now she liked children, how she began to wet herself. Her only response was a slow movement of the head. Other residents in the room ignored her except tall bald Eric who shut all the windows 'to keep the bairns out' and came and stood close to her chair and half took off his jumper.

Harry – at work – gave a little lurch towards me – couldn't help himself he always said – when he came through the door.

I wasn't stalking him, your honour.

He could teach me things, besides which books to read, there are things I don't know and need to. So many things, he could teach me politics, religion, laugh with me about my vicar husband, show me with his fingers and elbow back how to skim stones, he could teach Craig to swim.

He didn't know what was happening to him, he said, but he couldn't leave me alone, especially after the family fortnight abroad (Spain): he was at me, exuding waves of heat picked up and stored in his skin, almost indiscreet, snatching moments while the big fan whirred, while IT repaired our computers. I knew at lunch we'd be in his car. The afternoon meetings our thighs pressed together under the table – look no hands – turn up late or not turn up at all.

Tell her what he called her behind her back, the spit at his lips, the comfort I gave him that he took and took.

He praised my beauty my slimness my legs my spine even. My imagination when I haven't any. My smile, my smell. Want to hear his voice again, the small humming machine of it.

When I go to beat Adrian how shall I dress? What would be best to wear for ripping him to shreds, rip him to little crawling pieces, his skin and bones like insects running off?

To pay back the fear he's put in my poor Craig reduced to a whimpering blob in his bedroom not the sort of noise I want to hear from his door. After bullying him on social media: a WhatsApp group, Instagram, TikTok, things became real, things escalated. Craig returning in tears, I'm telling you, snotty, hair sweaty, some gunk in it, he didn't want to tell, but I got it out of him. Adrian using him as a punchbag, showing off to his mates, Craig shorter, hopeless. He is disappearing but doesn't want me to make a fuss. I see, I say, I understand, but, I tell him, setting my jaw, enough is enough. So, what would be best? You know I take my date dress down, don't you? You know I do my make up even more carefully, thinking of the later mugshots that might appear. How my unsmiling face and profile will blow up Twitter.

I've done the legwork, followed him, see the Evelyn in him: the stance, the gait, but the dad too, see which way he goes home which bit of urban brook he passes, maybe push him in, which I'm sure he did to Craig, although Craig says no, mum, I fell in. I've planned it out. The corner where he parts from his mates, where he can be tackled the large hedge hiding the business, the punch I will deliver and have practised on pillows propped on the sofa. Maybe with a fistful of keys.

I'll drag him by his ears as in those comics we read in the moonlight of our scruffy childhoods, hiding from our aunts who didn't like us reading. Here he is coming round that corner in his tall sandy world, knees that have dead legged Craig in dinner queues, sniffing to himself to hear the sound it makes on the apparently empty afternoon street. I will confront the lanky devil, I'll be fair though, I'll explain it may not be his fault with a mother like that before I hit him and hit him again.

LOW STAKES

THE END OF the story is the death of the reader. I don't like to get existential first thing but that's what I believe. When the reader stops reading they become something else – a worker, a slacker, a tyrant – or they pick up another story because that's their job or they've got too much time on their clock. Either way, the reader that read the last story has died, become someone else. And what of the characters? I believe they get reborn.

This is the crux. The plot of this story revolves around my destiny – my afterlife as a character. I refuse to end up in the bardo until the world decides it doesn't want to read stories anymore. Dog forgive I end up as an avatar in a videogame called something like *Skyhole: The Last of the Cloudbenders* or *Fake Deep 2: Avenging Our Artificial Ancestors*. I want to have feelings. I want to be self-aware. To ensure this, to my knowledge, I have to have good karma. To have good karma I have to do good deeds.

Now, I don't want to go overboard – I just want a normal next life. No one's going to play saint – this isn't that kind of story. I heard someone call the last Pope – what was his name? – 'GOD'S ROTTWEILER'. Who gets a nickname like that? Someone who is extremely suspect. 'God's Rottweiler' of the Jesus Mafia, squatting on the throne of the Vatican, fat with faith, melting with power. Nature's Gore-tex is righteous belief in the untouchable. This dog can do no wrong...

If I'm losing you, stick with it. All I'm saying is that all that saintly stuff – it's not my steez. I'm going for small acts of kindness to ensure an ordinary, relatively privileged but not overburdened afterlife. The intricate mechanisms behind the design I am not sure of. I can only have faith. It is the strength of this faith that I have to continuously reinforce.

Case in point: two nights ago I gave a woman £30. She'd had her phone and wallet stolen – that's all I could understand. She asked me my age and I told her 25. She said she had a daughter who was 26, a daughter who was 23, a daughter who was 21, all married with children. I said I had no chance of getting married. She kept crying and pleading with me, reaching into her handbag to show me a bracelet that she'd just picked up from Whitechapel. 'Two thousand pounds I paid for this and now I can't go home. Please, thirty pounds to get a taxi.' Well, everything happens for a reason. If I can afford to lose £30 then I suppose I'm expected to give it. Maybe I'd get a good return for it later on.

She was crying and hugging me, this tiny woman, and it felt rotten. A brief encounter turned sour by the exchange of money and my hidden motive for posthumous winnings. Well, I should've known it was a trick because this morning when I went out for a cigarette I noticed something in my rowboat. At first glance it looked like a coot had nested below the tarpaulin but on closer inspection it revealed the contents of my compost toilet, escaped from a ripped bin bag through foul play or otherwise. Everything happens for a reason, I suppose. Nose-deep in sawdust, loo roll, rainwater and floating turds, I confronted excretions made by a body that I'd inhabited after they were made. Was this a sign?

I've never betted on the horses, a nasty habit, but I'm partial to a £2 scratchcard. Low stakes. Maybe this will help you understand my predicament. Later on, after I'd cleaned all the shit out the rowboat, a man outside Co-op asked me for some change. I'd learnt my mistake from the night before and offered to buy him some bread and cheese – white and sliced. I didn't worry about getting myself anything as I was sure the story would be over soon. I felt better this time, giving away something as harmless as bread and cheese.

The walk back home was short, made long by the fact that I went to the shop and came back with nothing. As pavement moved beneath my feet, time splintered into regularly spaced fragments – moments in which isolated scenes presented themselves with symbolic meaning. In one, a boy blew vape rings, in another, a loudspeaker in the basket of a Santander bike played dubstep; in the last, a man in a mobility scooter decorated with Union Jack flags told me my home was on fire. It was only when I reached the towpath that I realised what he meant.

As in those moments when the heart sinks before the mind knows what's wrong, I acted as if nothing had happened. I took my keys out and stepped onto the boat, turning two different keys in three different locks. I stepped into the boat without seeing where I was going – there was smoke in my eyes – and thought about starting a fire. It was very warm for February and it looked as if the stove was already lit. The whole stove, and all the wood around it, was lit. As was the shelf adjacent, and the desk and the bench . . .

I have feelings like anyone else and this was my home, on

fire, on the water, and I had nowhere else to go. Dog knows I wanted to jump out into the canal and swim through the shit and microplastics to an unknown life. Instead I'm writing this while the insulation burns around me because all I have is my faith. I leave you with these words, until next time:

I take a peek through
My View-Master 5000 only
To realise at once that
I am blind. Pennies trickle
From my pockets and into
The fountain.
My wish is not to see
Clearly, but to
Perish peacefully in
The living light of faith.
By mixing Nature's ingredients
Over the fire I produce
Ancient spells of something
Unbodily and only then
Do I extinguish all hope
To remain.

STOCK

HE SAT INTEGRATED amongst the felled trees, cracked a crust of bark with just the barest pressure of his foot. The rabbits, compact shapes in the field above the cottage, unfolded pointed wings and scaled into the air, as if the bark's crack had sent them up.

It was stony cold. You are sleep deprived, he told himself. Not rabbits. They were never rabbits.

The tin panged as he got up the last forkful of uncooked beans. Chewed. Assessed the tubular timber not yet fetched from the slope. The countless downed trunks.

He'd read the notice, at the edge of the devastated plantation. Some disease he couldn't pronounce. 'A legal notice has been issued to fell these trees because they are infected.' And we already have the dieback, with the ash. They're cutting them too.

What would they do? The kites now were black motifs on the nearly morning sky. If we got some big illness. Some of us. Would they cut *us* down? Cull *us*?

The TB papers. His uncle's shaking hands.

Cuckoo spit. It's cuckoo spit next. He'd seen it on the

farming news. The little bugs that make it. Carrying some invasive thing. Some germ deadly to plants.

He looked around for puffs of froth on the thin growth that was coming up between the fallen larches. There's none. Too early. It's too early in the year. And then, finally, there was movement. A bar of light from the cottage.

He put the bean tin down, took the old brass telescope from his pocket. Click click, drew it to its length, raised it, unexpected chill against his eye.

Mrs Lewis Banc stood in the open doorway. With her apron on, bright and patterned, it looked like she peered over a border of small flowers.

Perhaps she sleeps in it. In a chair. Perhaps she sleeps in her clothes, like Nan.

Take them. He sent a message out to her. These are for you.

Mrs Lewis stared at the laden carrier bags before her on the path.

For you.

He sent a message out again, and now she stepped forward and bent. She picked up some food packets, held them for a moment as if they were things she didn't understand. Then she put them back, looked around, and carried the bags one by one into the house.

The door closed.

He scanned up and out beyond the cottage, to the more distant bwthyn on the hill, barely at the range of the scope, the carrier bags there just visible through the crossbars of the garden gate.

When he looked back to Mrs Lewis's cottage, he saw her

framed in the window, in the lights that were on in the kitchen, seated at the table, seemingly eye to eye with a pineapple, as if the fruit were something votive.

꧁

The sprung bell zonged mutedly as he came into the shop, the brush of the draught baffle across the wiry mat, the snip as the latch closed to.

He carried a vaporous energy from being awake all night.

The thin plastic dust sheets that had billowed gently when the door opened settled again against the shelves.

He looked at the carrier bags still left. The goods he had apportioned up. Caught sight of himself in the glass of the set-aside Post Office counter in the corner of the room. He didn't look the way he thought he looked.

She probably never had a pineapple that wasn't out of a tin.

He looked guilty and tired. Not as if he had done something good.

The glass-topped chest freezer gave an agitated hum. A sort of acknowledgement.

Mrs Lewis Banc.

Elin and Arwyn Cam Uchaf.

Edie Pen Cwm.

Maggie Tyddyn Llwyd.

Idris Bwlch.

They were always good to the shop. He mentally ticked them off.

The prip prip prip of postage stamps parting from their perforations. The thudunk of inking pension books.

Who else? Who else is left? Saw a map in his head.

The damping sponge, desiccated now, like a slice of stale toast.

He reached a milk from the open chiller. Jiggled it from between the cartons of fruit juice he hadn't yet shared out. Swigged. Felt a low burn in his finger creases against the cool plastic handle.

Flip-flop sound of making butter in a jar.

It's weak, this. Even the Full Fat. It's not like we had it. *The bottles achatter in the crates, the chickeny chatter of a chicken coop as Tadcu drove the van.* He still remembered the round. Which house came after which. The pull of lugging the bags in his upper arms.

He took one of the remaining old chocolate bars from beside the till, felt the till judge this act, blink, as the movement of his hand reflected in the black of its switched-off display. Tore the wrapper with his teeth. *Taste, the glue of stamps.* The chocolate pocked with tiny nets of air, paled marks. Wildly out of date.

Took stock.

There were the few over-the-counter medicines, sanitary items that embarrassed him.

The women's refuge would take them. He felt a twisting emotional pain – but I don't know exactly where it was, where she went – through his middle, and out. And then it was as if that pain trapped momentarily in the shop as the windows hummed, a recycling van pulled up outside, idled, and there was the clatter of glass. The van just a coloured patch through the drawn net curtains.

Let it go. Let it go. Eat, now. Get some sleep. Then, it's Wednesday, go and see Nan.

Mandy. She was always good. Would come with a list for Pencarreg too.

Pencarreg's gone though. Second home. Posh gravel. Solar panels.

The nearest would be Irfon, Maen Isaf. But he has the carers, now.

He assessed what was left again, the ready-loaded bags of refrigerated goods set there in the chiller.

Everybody has to have something.

Get some sleep. You'll be out again tonight.

The recycling van gurned, rattled, pulled away. The windows shook again.

I could just leave him dog food. The carers wouldn't notice that. Smoothed his hand habitually across the melamine as he passed behind the shop counter, went through into the rest of the house.

Every time he opened the driver's door he thought the same thing. I need to WD40 it.

He thought this time, just do it now, go in and get it and do it now, but then he thought of the hour-long drive ahead. Hour there, hour back.

He pulled the door closed, winced, even though he knew it

was coming, at the arthritic creak, but more in concern it would draw attention. *The graunch of the old cowshed doors.*

He thumbed the key and the engine woke with the sort of enthusiasm of an old dog offered a walk.

It's a good engine, just the body work. They said it every time. Body'll go before the engine. Made the same joke every time the MOT came round, 'got through on omissions'. He didn't really understand it.

The hour drive there and the hour drive back, and that he had to drive through town, made him nervous. It was the only time, he figured, the car might get flagged by the police. But he couldn't have Nan in a nearer home, there'd be too much coming and going, people who knew her.

꙰

   - Nan.

He put the carrier bags down in the kitchenette doorway.

   - Wednesday.

She looked at him, pleased, from the chair.

   - Half closing.

   - Yes, Nan.

   - A week, then, already.

Conversational, not a complaint. She had the chair faced into the flat, not at the window, not the placid grey screen of the television. At the photograph of his uncle and Tadcu and the cows coming in to the parlour to milk.

   - I could move your chair. If you want. To look out.

- No. I'm happy here.

He thought he could see for a moment the scene of the photograph reflect in her glasses but it was just the blacks and whites of the room.

- Shop busy?

- Always, Nan.

- Good to have the half day then.

- Yes. You can go in the day room, you know.

- I'm happy, *Bach*.

- I've brought some things. Do you want soup?

- Are you?

- I'll have something with you.

Slightly sick. Not enough food, not enough sleep. The low anxiety, the drive.

- I'll do soup. You can keep the meals on wheels for tea.

The tiny space trembled as a bus pulled into the stop outside, its throb swallowed in the double-glazing, different from the recycling van that morning.

- They don't stop, those. I don't know where people are going all the time.

He showed her the soup tins.

- Which do you want?

- They're different, these.

- They're the ones the suppliers had this week, Nan.

They're the same. Just different packets.

Her hands hovered.

- This is oxtail.

- Yes.

- If you'll have some as well then.

⚜

The meaty cow smell brought a queasy churn through his stomach. He was having trouble with the smell. Already the soup was agitating in the thin pan. Began to faintly hiss.

- No Mari again today, then.

- School, Nan. I told you. She's started half days. In the holidays maybe.

He pushed the kitchenette door part-closed to get at the unit behind, fetch out bowls and small plates. Stood up too fast.

- Mrs Evans Ty'n Banc still coming in?

- Every Thursday, yes. She always asks after you.

I'm not going to be able to eat this. Grey little lumps were surfacing and turning over on themselves in the pan.

- Six she's got.

He clattered the bowls. Fumped the fridge loudly open. Put the butter on the worktop.

There was an open packet of processed ham, thin discoloured slices. A small jug of milk. He lifted the ham as a pad.

- Six!

You have to eat. Still the sick feeling. You can't be up so long, carry stuff, on nothing.

He rolled the pad and ate it, shut the fridge with a receipting suck. A fleeting remembrance of that morning in his muscles.

- Car going well still?

- Going lovely, Nan.

He thought of the perishables lined up in the shop. Lifted the soup from the electric hob. Poured it into the bowls. Found sliced bread.

He heard the soft roll of Nan's chair table as she got it in place, wheels over the inexplicable wiry carpet tiles.

- I'll do toast.

The photograph of the cows was stuck in his mind. The high hips of the Holsteins. The cowshed.

The window rumbled again as he reached spoons from the drainer, spacked the drawer open and transferred things into the cutlery tray, scraped dried missed scabs of food off with his nail.

It was the first sign. Things not washed properly. Lids not properly on the jam she made, tiny blooms of mould. These things at first he put down to her eyes.

He had a fleet, horrible thought of her being cleaned, the ladies that came. *Phop*, toast. Scraped on butter. A muted hiss as the bus moved away.

Tadcu, in the photo. Tadcu, he wouldn't have coped.

When he'd taken the food through and knew Nan would

not leave the chair he took the carefully kept foil top from his jacket pocket, ran his thumb around inside the disc to slightly splay the rim.

He lifted the milk carton from the carrier bag still in the doorway and quietly took it over to the sink, slid over the cleaned glass bottle she'd put beside the draining board. Then he poured the carton milk into the pint bottle and fitted the foil top on.

He couldn't help himself glance through the kitchenette door, to Nan. To check.

Her hands were lifted slightly as she sat, fingers moving as if they worked an unseen till, but she was gazing at the picture of Tadcu, Uncle and the cows. Came back when the filled bottle clinked, as he put it into the door compartment, called through.

- There's the clean bottle for you by the sink.

- Yes, Nan. Got it, thanks. I've put a new one in the fridge.

- Uncle well?

- He's fine.

- Milk round.

- Yes, Nan. He'd like to come and see you but. He's on his own with the cows.

- Yes, he'll be busy.

- Always busy, yes.

- Always the same, with cows.

- Yes, Nan. Always the same. Everything's the same.

Everything's still the same.

⁂

- Thank you for stopping.
- Fine, Ifan, really. Slow job on your own.

Ifan's spanned hand sunk into the fleece at the ewe's pilled haunch, pressed, read the grade of muscle.

- Still going, then.

The car was up on the verge beside the handling area, there beside the road.

- Should never have sold her!

Ifan let the ewe into the left-hand bay.

- Bargain for you there, your Nan got.

The sheep Ifan had graded so far were all in that bay. The right bay was empty.

- Nineteen, *ni'n eisau*. Why not a round twenty I don't know.

He showed the next ewe down the race to Ifan.

- Always fuss, with sheep. Not so much fuss, cows.

Ifan looked up and out as he pressed his hand to the new ewe, visualising the dressed-out carcass. He was looking up visualising, but it seemed he looked at the bright truck that made its way along the single-track road to the chapel clad with scaffold on the opposite hill.

- We won't have to grade them all this rate.

Ifan let the ewe also into the left-hand bay.

- Good spring.

- Not so much that. Just, I've got less animals now.
  Less animals on the same grass, *ti'mod?*

He nodded at Ifan. Ifan seemed to catch himself up, then.

- Sorry to mention the cows like that. Then. I didn't
  mean to bring your uncle up for you.

He dismissed it. As if it was nothing. Dug his grip into the
next sheep's wool as she went stubborn, felt a faint rip of
fleece when he hefted her.

The percussive smack of hammering came over from the
chapel.

I can't really picture that, what has to be done to the inside
of a chapel to make it somewhere to live in. Thought of
the farmhouse. How long would it be before it was sold?
Snapped up and its insides stripped out to make a country
place for someone. Couldn't stop then the thought of
stripped-out innards and there was nothing there, when
they opened them up, no lesions, but still they had to
slaughter the herd, the whole herd, after generations.

- Daughter, you too, isn't it?

He nodded again. The lichen on the breeze block race.
Splayed patches. *No signs. There were no signs, nothing on
the lungs.*

- Two, see. Better, I think. Grown up now, though.
  I might have pushed a boy into the farm. I'm glad,
  mewn ffordd.

Ifan received the stubborn ewe.

You'll be another one. You'll work yourself into nothing and then the farm will get eaten up by a rich farm.

- This one too! No surprise mind. Been waiting three weeks to book them in.

No wonder they're grading. His nails burned from pulling at the stubborn ewe.

- What is it, two hours?

- Two hours there, yes. Bit quicker on the way back. With the trailer empty.

Then hours more, to some supermarket butchery, to be put into packets and driven round again. Could even end up back on our doorstep.

The next sheep hovered, leant against the breeze block channel, reluctant to move. He made some primitive noises. Clicked to her. Then he spotted her held-up foreleg.

He leant into the race to get behind the ewe, encourage her on her awkward front leg, felt the bruise in the centre of his palm again as he held his weight on the blocks.

- Bad foot, this one.

The smell of the unhealthy ewe filled his nose. He tightened his mouth as if that would close up his nostrils. Strongarmed her along. Brought a wash of tiredness up him, a loose empty feel, so when Ifan received the hurt ewe and expertly turned her over and sat her up, as if there was no effort in it at all, he couldn't connect it up, the strength.

He got over the hurdle to help hold the ewe, lifted the injured foot.

Ifan dug muck from the concave of the protruded hoof, flicked it off the clippers, bit at the big nail with the blades. Then he spread the toes. His face changed. A quiet patient revulsion.

The stink came up between the toes and out. The compact cream-coloured boil of clotted pus popped with the smallest nick, the ewe bridling as Ifan scraped a small hard node out with the clipper points and the stinking paste of rot globbed down the foot.

He turned from the stench. Turned his head away, felt oxtail bile. It was the smell. That smell. He was trying to hold away the stench of the pus, the decay. More, he was trying to hold away what was coming from it.

He looked down at his palm, pocked from the pressure of the breeze blocks. Thought guiltily of the dented shotgun stock. Maybe I could iron it out. Soak the stock and iron it.

   –   She's gone backwards, this one.

Ifan could tell just from handling her.

   –   We'll let her off.

The ewe started kicking. Pedalling into the air. Like to protest this wasn't the fate she wanted. He leant in. Tight wires of wool on her white face. A watery spit of chewed grass. Bright phlegm. There was a notch out of her ear, as if she'd already been marked out.

Ifan hissed spray onto the splayed foot, asked with his eyes down, as he checked the other feet.

   –   Is your uncle's barn better?

It was as if thinking about the stock had brought the question, about the borrowed gun. They'd taken his uncle's away, after.

  – Yes.

He couldn't look at Ifan. Knew he was fond of the old gun.

  – Thanks for the lend.

The truck had arrived now at the chapel and the delivery men were unloading a bathroom suite, setting it congregated in front of the door. The ewe's unnaturally blue one foot pointed up to them in exclamation.

  – Good little gun for rats, four ten.

☕

The brass scope felt different in his hands, with his skin supple from the lanolin.

He checked the time again.

She should be back. They should be back by now. Half day. She should be home.

She could have walked. If the old school was still there. An architects' office now. Same architects doing the chapel. If she didn't have to go to the big shiny new school. She could have just walked. Like I did. Or go on her bike. *Learning to ride on the yard, his uncle's hand steadying the seat.* It's a forty-five-minute run.

No point coming home, in between lifts, for a half day. You'd just have to turn around.

He picked one of last year's crab apples from the ground,

shrunk and wrinkled, rolled it in his hand. Pushed distract-
edly against it. Thought of the puckered knuckles of the
pineapple. Nan's hands. Kept his eyes on the far-off
road.

It's been an hour. Since she finished. More than an hour.

Bramble was coming into leaf. Lambs bleated across the hill.
There was a skylark somewhere.

They're late.

He looked at the road as if he could draw their car onto it.
He was trying to hold down a sick nervous feeling. Could
taste the oxtail soup.

⚘

When the car came along he found it in the scope, held it in
the circle of the lens as Annie parked at the bungalow, got
out, and Mari burst from her seat in the back, ran to kick
her football.

A relief waved through him. Just the sight of her.

He had the strange sensation sometimes that the scope itself
held Mari. That the world she existed in was *within* the
scope. That he could fold the scope down, if he chose to,
and carry her away with him.

But I wouldn't. I am not like that. I'd never, whatever they
think.

He pushed his heels into the small ridge his feet had formed
in the slope after months of him coming there. A mark of
place, like the worn patch of lino beneath his chair in the
kitchen, his place, ever since Mam had gone, where he'd sat

since he was a child, his legs growing year by year down to the floor until they reached, as if putting down roots.

I got angry, but I could never. Not that.

He imagined the thuds of the ball against the bungalow wall, the zip of the boot as Annie opened it, lifted out some bags for life.

Of course, he understood. That's why they're late. They'll have had to go for shopping.

Mini peppers. Cucumber. Shiny veg. He saw the list in his head. It's shiny, all that veg.

꧁

He opened the lock knife and marked in another groove. The old fence post was bleached, the greyed of the felled trunks that morning.

He was about to stand and head away, drop out of sight and follow the rill to where he'd left the car on the other side of the hill, by a slope of recently planted trees, none taller than the guards around them. But as he pushed the lock tab and closed the knife, leant his weight forward a little to rise, the police car arrived at the bungalow.

Immediate sweat, a stomach churn. His palms oil as two police got from the car. What? Annie at the door before they knocked. Bones of a sudden watery, as if he was unmixing.

He hesitated as he lifted the scope, hand midway through the action, in a gesture that looked aimed to stop something. Warn.

He felt the urge to run. At the same time felt drilled into place.

She can't know. Lifted the scope. Tried to find conviction he would hear through it. She can't have seen me.

They cannot know.

A notebook flicked. A scribbled pen. Annie's ponytail shook. No. A brief scratch in the quickthorn made the sound of the pen's nib, Mari's small face, pressed at the window. No. They cannot know.

Her face right against the glass, then the big sky reflected, as if it came out of her head.

Thumps of adrenalin now.

He thought of everyone knowing. Felt fear. *Thought* of fear, the spate of raids on Post Offices, do not worry, Nan and Tadcu all those years back, *do not worry*. Shotguns. Balaclavas. Of what it would be like to be amongst the products, the shopping, and face a gun and have to really cower. To pray.

Of the police coming.

He felt sick and full of metal. Watched the police walk back to their car, open the doors, get in and drive away.

※

He met the police car as he rounded the lake. Saw the car on the opposite shore, the clean white of the turbines beyond, the low rushes stepping out into the water, two geese folded in the shallows and the sky held in the surface, Mari and the sky like her mind in the window.

Bryn Oerfa. They've been to Bryn. That's the only place up there.

He understood then. They're going house-to-house.

He slowed and pulled in. One of only a few places cars could pass on the narrow road. The gateway cut with quad-bike ruts, so the car sat uneasily.

He waited. Bloomed with heat again. A slight chill immediately meeting the edges of his sweat. His neck vein thick, suddenly. Too small.

The worst rusted side won't show. Not how the car is in the gateway like this. They won't look, he told himself. That's not what they're doing, here. They've got better things to do than notice an old car.

The other car neared at a steady, measured pace. As if it didn't want to spook him.

Sit. It's just panic. A fish in his chest. Remember what the doctor said. Say thank you. Thank you, body, for warning me, but it's okay. It's nothing. It is not a lion.

For an insane moment he believed he would spin the car around, flee, or ram the police into the water. Take off on foot.

How would they find me? Dogs? It would be the only way. A hammer percussion in his chest.

But they can't know. Calm yourself. They cannot know yet what it is I am doing.

He looked through the gateway, at the ruts that continued away into the field, a track that had been set.

Briefly, the police car was out of sight behind a lobe in the road, and then it reappeared, slowed, the police waved him an acknowledgement, and passed on with a nod.

⁂

He got only a few metres before he had to stop the car again, the horrible graunch of the car door, *the cowshed door*, got out and was sick. Hands on knees. Biled. A two-tone slug of goose shit. Blue condom wrapper in the grass. A burst of feathers, closely scattered, fallout of some bird taken as prey.

When the sing of endorphin died back, the air thumped with the turbines, the beat on the breeze from the far ridge, *thwock thwock*, an under-roar that fell into time with his decelerating pulse.

And then he laughed – you mad bastard! Delightedly. You're mad. You're cracked. They do not know. Midges whined above his vomit. Obviously. They do not know – was still laughing when he had to get back in the car and reverse out of the way of a smart people carrier, a family, so he guessed, coming for a stay in the lovely countryside.

⁂

He held his hands in the cool edge of the river, flexed his fingers. They looked abnormally white in the tan water. The red marks of the carrier bags disappeared.

He was still and engrossed in his hands.

When he looked up, birds had come to drink at a shallow beach across the way. Orange-red, or green-yellow. They were birds he'd never seen before, and in the strange liminal state that early in the morning, they did not seem quite real. They dipped, lifted, tiny clicks, made subdued *djeeps*, the sound of a squeezy dog toy.

When he moved, the birds scattered.

The contained *cuff* of the falls filled the place. Glassy peals of broken water.

There was no green at all on the oaks, tight closed on the steep sides of the gorge. Still late to open.

I'll get up high, through them. Up to the top to see the road.

Birdsong had burst the quietness of the woodland as he'd followed the cwm down. One lone bird, then myriad, as if in praise of him. Less a chorus, more a drumming, an incantation.

By the time he reached the falls, perhaps only because of the previous ceremonial intensity of the song, it had come to feel strangely quiet.

That's something they made fun of, when I was little. He used to think the sun rose because the birds called to it, sang it up.

No-one disabused him. Then he went to school.

It's merciless, school. They tell you it's training for life, but it's not. It's not anything like life.

He studied how his skin looked unnatural in the water, closed his sore hand on a submerged stone that fitted as if designed into his palm. It looked an amphibious colour. Surprised him when it wasn't slick. Take it with you. He lifted it.

Use a stone this time.

His hands were icy. He shook the water from them, then dried them on the woollen balaclava.

The resin the water had not washed off his skin tacked to the fibres. There was that and the lanolin oils from handling the sheep.

The sweat of manhandling the fallen tree hung damp now in his T-shirt. A cold patch under his jumper, stuck against his back.

What are you doing?

The eyeholes of the balaclava seemed just then to gawp at him. Ask disbelief.

No. You do this. It must be done. People need to see. That if things don't stop everything will just be gone, will go. And we will not get it back.

Even the pubs have gone. Chapels. Now the schools.

The little shop.

No.

Stop.

A shiver went through him. A reset.

The orange-red and green-yellow birds had come back. Djeeped. Supplicating to the water.

Everybody on the list. Everybody who helped the shop. Everyone who was kind. Everyone who misses Nan.

Stop.

Don't fall into that angry thing, now. Get it done.

He picked up the bag. The birds scattered again. He looked up through the oaks.

Get done what you have told yourself you are going to do.

⚜

A crisp green salad and shell-on prawns.

He kept the supermarket delivery van centred in the scope. It seemed to stall almost, to make the awkward turn up and on to Ffosffin.

It's like a toy. It's like a toy van. It's like a happy little van on children's telly.

The cardboard box under the stairs, with the fire engine, the taxi, racing cars, and the plastic trucks, people figures bigger than vehicles, out of size, giants.

He read the inane cheery claim on the boxy back of the van, watched as the vehicle throttled down on the lane, took the bend, past the handling area, Ifan's sheep, and went out of sight.

⚜

Ten minutes at Ffosffin with the delivery. They unload the shopping into a wheelbarrow and take it back and forth. Then a few minutes to loop back down the lane to the road.

He'd dropped down off the rise, through the geometric plantation, the soft-cushioned underfoot needled floor, followed the little spots of marker-spray on the trunks to the loose tree he'd left balanced in the early hours.

He strained to listen through the passive *hush* the breeze put through the conifers.

Nothing. Not yet.

Then, little *djeeps* broke the hush, *djeep djeep*, the birds, them, now again, busy, drew his eye to see frail tawny flakes helicoptering around him, nipped from the cones they busied at, *tiny upside-down pineapples.*

He put out a hand but the flake he aimed to catch sailed from the movement, displaced like a small object in water.

And as the flake found the ground, he heard the van.

Its specific motor sound amplified in its tinny carcass.

Yes.

The birds broke away as he moved, his weight against the levered tree, so barely held, spun, so that with one roll, a hard bite into his shoulder and with a creak more metalish than timber the trunk lurched off the slope, snapped an artilleral *crack* as it met the tarmac surface, reared once, and fell still. As the motor sound developed, tone-change, lowered gurn as the van geared down in anticipation. Just around the corner.

He rolled the balaclava, raised the gun, and stepped into the road.

꧁

When he lifted his hands from the steering wheel, they tacked slightly.

He turned off the engine and, for a moment, there was an intense peace.

He unhooked his left foot from under the seat, stretched it in the space he'd expect to find the clutch.

He took a breath. A moment. Prodded the vehicle tracking device like you might a small dead animal, to check it was really dead. Felt the sharp upturned lip in the plastic where he'd smashed the lock knife in, this time with the river stone. Squeezed his fingers into a fist to feel what he thought almost was yesterday's deserved dull pain in the centre of his hand.

Then he got out and graunched shut the cowshed door, and the place fell into dimness.

It made the other delivery van that was there seem to lurk.

It held him, unnervingly, as he let his eyes adjust. Then he went back to the van he'd just parked, and reached the .410 from the footwell. Perhaps sensing him, the man locked in the goods bay of the van began desperately to shout.

He steeled himself, put back on the balaclava, threateningly bashed the concertinaed side.

- Enough. I'm going to open the hatch. Don't say anything.

The roller side crattled up. The driver was on his knees, gripping the shelves as if the van was still travelling.

- Out.

The driver gripped the shelves like to let go of them would cause him to fall. Like he would drop.

- Out.

He kicked down the foldable step.

In some daze, the driver moved, slowly climbed out. The thickened rubber soles of his shoes looked remedial. Toyish, like the van itself.

The driver was cramped and shaking. His lip jabbered. When he saw the other van, a pathetic sob went through him.

- There's no money.

- Have any people brought freezer bags?

The driver didn't understand.

- Someone's bought freezer bags?

They had. Several people had.

- All the stuff with the supermarket name on. Go crate by crate. In a packet with the supermarket on. Take it out. Take it out of the packaging and put it into freezer bags. If they are tins and things you can't do that with put them to one side.

The thick lenses of the driver's glasses went briefly opaque.

That's what happens. It's what happens at the moment an animal dies. Its eyes go out.

He raised the shotgun. Felt the pattern of the wool in his skin as he pressed the stock to his cheek.

- Please.

- Crate by crate. Separate everything out.

He couldn't smell the cowshed through the balaclava. Just the damp clothes smell. He couldn't feel the dryness of the cowshed. He was sweating. His hands slick on the gun.

There was the sweat, and the grease of the lanolin, and the resin tack, and the starch effect of the grain, from when he'd swapped out the lead from the cartridges.

It was nearly done.

- Not the bottled water. Keep some toilet roll.

The driver was on his knees amongst the boxes. Packaging strewn, blatant. The driver's childish thickened upturned soles.

- Tuna. Do you like tuna?

Tight dapples of light came now through the clustered holes the shot had made in the galvanised wall behind the chair when his uncle pulled the trigger. Bright solid pellets.

He tried to block the thought out.

Tried to unhear the detail, the flies. He shouldn't know. The holes. He couldn't dislodge the thought, they'd eaten through the wall to get in. To get at him.

Stop.

- Tuna.

A discarded bakery item bag uncurled on the floor, as if of its own accord. As if it would unravel and scuttle across the cowshed floor.

The driver looked incoherent. Again a sob, more a choke, came up.

He checked the own-brand cans to see they had ring pulls. Bananas. A bag of already chopped carrots. Own-brand sliced loaf.

- Jam?

The driver was crying now. Full-on crying.

- Do you want jam?

He passed in the torch and brought down the roller side.

There was a sudden silence in the cowshed.

The hair on his nape stiffened.

It felt the silence came profoundly from, was generated actually by the other van.

He gazed at the re-sorted goods. Re-bagged meat, grey through thin blue plastic. The discarded packaging across the ground, *strewn feathers from a taken bird*. Slim scattered straw. A desiccated pellet of cow cake, *goose shit*.

And then a sobbing broke out from the latest van by which he still stood. A sort of bovine moan. Then a sudden din. A crazy batter. Like the clang of a loose gate. A noise that cracked at his skull. The white bonnet. *White police car*, a sudden compression, overtaking, doubt buzzed. The horrible flies.

- Enough!

The light through the holes in the wall fell in rods, white tunnels of dust.

- Enough!

The deep silence came back. Again seemed to come from the other van.

He went over. Approached as if the van would shy, or bolt, kick out like an unnerved animal.

Why is he so quiet? He was mad yesterday, he raged.

He patted the roller door with the butt of the shotgun. Nothing. Sailed for a moment on a horrible soupy uncertainty. Tried to secure himself to the ground. Then he undid the latch, *it's not a lion*, barrels levelled as the door scaled up.

The stink of shit and urine hit him. Came through his uncovered mouth, came as taste.

The driver squatted crouched on the diminished case of sparkling water bottles. He'd more or less demolished the inside of the bay. Gouged where he'd tried with the frames of the racks to lever away the side panels. His hands cut.

Blood dried on the van floor. Crusted on his uniform.

The driver looked so slight, even in the tiny goods bay. His body contorted between the mangled lengths of angled metal.

The driver just stared. Stared at the gun. Looked back at him with blank disgust.

He relowered the door. Lifted off the balaclava. Everything was spinning now. Try to get a hold. It's choice. It's a choice. You've done this.

Everyone on the list. You have to do everyone on the list. If nothing more.

Thought of Nan. Thought of the wiry carpet tiles, the blunt nose of the struggling ewe. Tried to grip some detail from the day to hold to. Like the doctor'd said. Green-yellow birds. The bags. The stacks. Taken stock. Boxes all around the floor.

But the cowshed was alternately compressing, shrinking and expanding, chasmic. The walls.

He looked up at the spattered holes, the tight dots of light. *They ate him. They came in and ate him.*

- What do we do now? What are you going to do now?

The driver's shouted question echoed in the van. Contained. Words clattered. Flies.

- What now?

In his head. Little holes.

- What happens?

Burst out.

Spinning.

- What?

Spinning.

- What happens now?

CHARLOTTE TURNBULL

HEADSHOT

THE DAMAGE TAKES place in a glamorous location. When the new assistant looks up at the building, Soho's skinny, smoky streets seem to lean towards her new office. It is like the pin at the centre of London's compass; the pivot of a whole city. There is an unlikely Rowan tree growing from the pavement in front of it. While the city's plane trees were deliberately planted to withstand pollution, the rowan will have seeded naturally. Where the new assistant comes from, rowans will cultivate inhospitable soil, providing shelter for other saplings - oaks, beeches - which then colonise, thriving once the hard work is done, and eventually dwarfing the rowans. Thinking happily of the moor, the new assistant thinks the rowan is a good sign.

She swipes her card to open the automatic glass doors on the ground floor and thinks she hears the whip of rush-hour heels behind her stop, for a moment, as people notice where she's going - as they see the actors and actresses staring, moody and flawless, from the posters in the lobby.

But when the new assistant steps out of the lift onto the correct floor, the ceilings are low. The carpets are threadbare and it smells of urine. From reception, she looks towards offices that can only be reached through passages narrowed by explosive shelves of boxes and files and scripts.

The new assistant understands why she was not interviewed here, at the office.

She had met her future boss, Francesca, at an exclusive, members-only club. She waited on a scuffed Chesterfield in front of a mug-stained farmhouse coffee table where her plastic wallet of handwritten notes and pre-prepared questions looked both litigious and childish at once. The other patrons spoke in low voices and wore jeans and shirts and Converse that somehow all shone like pelts. But, during the interview, Francesca laughed at the new assistant's jokes, with a loud, unselfconscious bellow. Francesca turned heads. She caught eyes with people who waved and smiled. The new assistant believed everyone wished they were in her meeting, having fun.

There are books of renovation plans in reception for the talent to look at. The new assistant flicks through one while she waits to be shown to her desk. On the glossy cover, a jarring photoshopped blue sky hangs above the building, precarious, like it is dangling by strings. In the photograph, the mirrored windows make the building look somehow cleaner than any building is, or can be - there is no tree in the pavement, let alone a rowan. The assistant turns the page and the interiors gleam - polished floorboards; glinting, empty desks; white, blind computer monitors. There is a computer-generated glint from the glass of framed mock posters covering the walls. Each pretend film is complete with badges of fictional awards.

Wow, the new assistant thinks, one day this place will be perfect.

It is the new assistant's first task every morning to collect and tabulate viewing figures and box-office statistics for all the company's productions, and those of their competitors. The company keeps a close eye on how everyone else is performing.

On her first day, Francesca waits at the new assistant's desk, while she prints out a copy of the weekend's stats. The Managing Director joins her and slowly other executives are drawn to her desk, like sharks to chum. The Managing Director asks the new assistant to pronounce her name, twice.

'I'll never remember that.' He takes the printout from the printer, still warm, and flicks quickly through at the statistics. 'You're Dave.'

Francesca rolls her eyes and grins at Dave.

'He's a nightmare,' she says, kindly.

Dave is flattered to be part of an in-joke, grateful to have her dream job.

The other executives point numbers out to one another, watching for the Managing Director's reaction. When the Managing Director leaves, he shoves the papers, now cooling, into the bin. The other executives follow suit.

Dave arrives early, before Francesca, each day.

The runners and interns are in even earlier. The photocopiers need to warm up. They check and replace toner, paper. The dog room needs airing; fresh bowls of water, clean rugs for the dog beds. Dave thinks that the industry press should do a 'Star Dogs of Tomorrow' list, alongside the lists published for the agents, producers, writers, directors, but she never says it out loud. Dave and the other asthmatic assistants keep their inhalers close.

The assistants arrive next. Monitors flash on instantly across the floor – no one ever powers down completely, just in case. Foil-wrapped breakfast orders sweat on their tables. There is a queue for the small office kitchen. People empty low-fat yoghurt and blueberries into bowls, chop lemons for hot water, microwave rice porridge.

Assistants join the company tall and confident from drama schools; pigeon-toed and broke from literature MAs; chaotic and assured from the families of well-known directors, producers, actors. The other assistants like to talk about plays or films they've just seen. They want to talk about weaknesses of scripts, and poor choices of cast. Dave loves to listen to them while she does her work. They are clever, insightful. It is a pity, she thinks, that they are only speaking to one other.

'What did you do before this?' Dave asks the assistant sitting opposite her who they all call Alan.

'Nothing,' Alan says, without looking up. 'I did nothing.' She waves Dave away with one hand. Dave notices she is missing half of her little finger.

Dave and the other assistants sit in the open-plan heart of the floor, surrounded by the executive offices. Their bodies are hidden from each other by low cubicle walls. The executives have windows – views across the city – and access to a balcony running around the edge of the building, 17 storeys high; they smoke there after hours, in expensive, sparkling sunsets.

All day, the assistants sit away from the natural light, in strip-lit dark. In the height of summer, Dave wonders, if she were able to look down from the balcony, would she see the rowan below her? Would its ripening fruit look like someone's chucked a handful of red sequins at it?

In the board room, at the end of Dave's first weekly company meeting, an assistant called Graham puts her hand up.

'Someone's blocked our emergency exit,' she says, 'with boxes of old DVDs.'

'The refurbishment,' the Managing Director says. 'We'll deal with *all* that in the refurbishment.'

After a week in this office, Dave realises the Managing Director means the carpet runners that peel up causing the assistants to trip and stumble daily. He means the taps overshooting the small, individual sinks that make the assistants' bathroom floor slippery. He means cords snaking across the floor around the photocopier.

'But, what if there's a fire?' Graham says.

The Managing Director looks too serious. 'We put fires out in this company, darling.'

The executives all laugh at the joke.

'We could give them to charity,' Graham says, quietly, pretending to take a note. 'If no one wants them anymore.'

The executives watch the Managing Director watching Graham.

'Good idea.' The Managing Director sighs. 'We must do what we can for charity.'

The executives nod slowly at what has turned out to be a good idea.

Graham looks like she's trying not to smile.

The first time Dave gets hurt, the Managing Director is

walking down the narrow passage with the film star, Jeremy Jones. Dave almost walks into them with a fresh cup of coffee for Francesca.

'Woah,' Jeremy Jones shouts. He has a briefcase cuffed to one wrist that he lifts up with both hands as he swings around to avoid her. Not a drop of coffee is spilt.

'Jesus,' says the Managing Director. 'Slow down, Dave.'

'I'm too valuable for burns.' Jeremy Jones smiles, but, for some reason, Dave feels sick. 'It's OK, darling.' He reaches out a hand. It slides from Dave's elbow to her wrist, which feels snappable in his grip. 'I'm OK, darling,' Jeremy Jones says, although, it is Dave who would have been scalded.

'Sorry.' Francesca comes down the passage and takes the cup from Dave. She stands in front of Dave; she blocks Dave from view. 'She's new.'

Francesca and Dave turn sideways, pressing back into the files and boxes to allow the Managing Director and Jeremy Jones through into reception. The briefcase runs over Dave's thighs briefly. Dave can't *not* look at it. The metal casing is smeared, greasy. After they have passed, Dave thinks she can smell something rotting, and brushes off her legs, assuming it is one of the dogs.

'What's in the briefcase?' Dave whispers to Francesca, as they walk back to their desks.

'None of your business.' Francesca sucks her cheeks in until her lips square together, blunt as a mallet.

Another executive crosses the office and leans against Francesca to speak in a low voice. 'How,' she says, 'has *he* not been cancelled yet?'

'I know,' Francesca says. The narrow passage way is like a telescope as they watch Jeremy Jones in reception. He runs a finger back and forth over the cuff around his wrist, as he speaks to the Managing Director.

Francesca reaches out to take a document from Dave's desk and seems to stumble slightly, pouring her entire cup of boiling coffee onto Dave's lap. Dave only registers a moment after the steaming liquid has soaked through her thin, polyester trousers onto the skin of her thighs. She stands up, fast, and pulls the wet fabric from her legs. She can't believe it happened.

'And what is in that *disgusting* briefcase?' Francesca brings her cup to her face, hugging it with her whole hand like it is precious - kissing its lip - looking from Dave to the other executive with playful eyebrows.

Dave smiles at Francesca. Dave knows Francesca is under a lot of pressure and assumes that Francesca had not seen her there; not remembered she had hot coffee in her hand; didn't realise what she'd done.

Francesca looks into her mug, and sees it empty.

'Could I have another, please?' She places the cup back onto Dave's desk and both executives go, arms folded, lips hard, back into their respective offices.

Dave stares at her hot, damp lap, then at the floor. She looks for a piece of curling carpet, but sees nothing to explain the sudden trip. Somehow, she thinks, the executives always know exactly where to tread.

When she looks up again, Alan is using powder to cover up a bruise on her cheek bone.

It is a busy fortnight. Dave encourages Francesca to go home when her head drops slowly in front of her computer screen. Dave makes a joke of walking backwards, waving paperwork like a carrot so Francesca will leave her office, to stagger into the lift, into the cab waiting for her at the entrance of the building.

Dave, herself, can't afford a cab, or the hours lost to night buses. She sleeps on the sofa in the dog room; sometimes on the sofa in Francesca's office when the dog room is taken by another assistant. In the mornings, the assistants give each other privacy to strip-wash in the leaky bathroom. Afterwards, they each mop up the floor with the thin ply toilet tissue and Dave learns to keep fresh underwear in her drawer, between the energy drinks and tampons. None of the assistants mention this to their bosses, not since they were all given a serious warning about using the office outside office hours – apparently the company is not covered for this by their health and safety insurance.

After another late night, Francesca comes into the office at lunchtime. She stands behind Dave's chair, smelling of alcohol. Francesca strokes Dave's long hair, smooths it across Dave's shoulders, and then invites her into a meeting.

'We've got to give you development opportunities,' Francesca says. 'You can't keep shuffling paper forever.'

Dave glances across to the other assistants, hoping someone else has heard this.

Dave is excited. She reads every draft of every script that comes into Francesca's inbox, in her own time though – in the evenings, at weekends, on holidays – because on work time she is supposed to be handling the diary, or running out to get Francesca's lunch and dry cleaning. The meeting is about a thriller, but a quiet one. It's one of those stories, she thinks, where the story isn't really about what the story is about.

During the meeting, neither Francesca nor the casting

director looks at Dave. Dave takes notes and, eventually, asks the age range for the female lead.

'Why has she gone so red?' Francesca nods at Dave, but looks at the casting director, smiling. 'Are you nervous or something?' she says, spreading a pile of headshots across the floor with one toe.

'I don't know, Francesca.' Dave's voice breaks out high. She truly doesn't know, but realises she is, now, blushing.

The casting director twists a glossy black and white photograph of a famous actor, back and forth between his hands.

'The problem is,' the man says, suddenly throwing it to the floor with the rest, 'the problem is I wouldn't fuck her.'

'Yes,' says Francesca, sounding tired. 'That is the problem. Dave, can we have some lunch?'

By the time Dave returns with two bespoke salads, the meeting is over, the casting director has gone, and Francesca is compiling contracts at Dave's desk.

'I'm not too good to do my own stapling,' Francesca says mildly, when Dave tries to take over. So, instead, Dave collects the papers into the correct order and holds them straight, while Francesca staples.

Francesca lines the stapler up again and, looking out into reception, she leans her full weight onto it, before Dave has a chance drawn her hand away. A pin of the staple runs through the soft, thin stretch between Dave's thumb and first finger.

Dave shakes her hand slightly, like she might just shake the document off. She realises that her body is now part of a signatory copy of a contract, and she thinks she might faint. But when she looks up for help, Francesca is back in her office, leaving Dave to do the rest of her stapling.

There are perks - the odd premiere, parties, a set visit, once - but no one ever wants to speak to Dave at those things and Dave never receives a plus one. She learns to hug the walls at events, pretending to send emails. Dave's friends always ask about it - the nurses, the teachers, the solicitors - they always want to know who she's met; she's better than the *Daily Mail* app, they tell her. But Dave's actual favourite thing about her job is that, from her desk, she can see the reception area. She can watch actors, directors and other *talent* sit there, checking their phones, staring into space, behaving like normal people. For some reason, no one ever asks about the ripped sofas. They seem content to ignore the nervy smell of dog urine.

Dave emails her friends, as a group, the day an actor they all love is coming into the office. They know her from a science fiction show they had watched together at university. The actor moved back home from Los Angeles to London, Dave tells her friends, after the show ended suddenly.

Before the meeting Francesca watches an episode of the show in her office.

'This is a good one,' Dave says, from Francesca's doorway. 'This one is good.'

'You really have to know what you're doing with sci fi,' Francesca says, shaking her head, leaning back in her chair and sighing.

'They did,' Dave says.

'They didn't,' Francesca says, looking at Dave, laughing at her. 'Because they were cancelled.'

After the meeting, Francesca shows the woman out of her

office and Dave asks her to sign one of the headshots they've been sent by her agent.

'Ah, sweet.' Francesca pats Dave on the back, and smiles at the actor. The actor signs the headshot, distracted, and Francesca leads her out into reception.

Dave pins the headshot above her desk, but when Francesca returns, she pulls the shredder out from under Dave's desk.

As Francesca pulls the headshot off the wall, she somehow gets her fist tangled in Dave's hair. She turns the shredder on and shoves the headshot through it, hair and all.

Dave's neck clicks as she realises what has happened. Her head is dragged down, and Francesca has gone back into her office. Not wanting to draw the office's attention, Dave grabs blindly, silently, to switch the shredder off, quickly pulling the power cord out at the back.

As the shredder whirrs down, the actor comes back to Dave's desk and looks down at her.

'Would you mind calling me a cab, sweetheart?' she says.

Dave twists around on the floor to sit up, head still inches from the metal teeth. She picks up the shredder to balance it on her lap, to sit at the desk and reach for her headset. 'Please have a seat in reception. I'll come and get you when the cab's here.'

Later, at her desk, her remaining hair clipped up, Dave has replies in her inbox from her friends. How was it? they ask. Did you speak to her? Did you do the salute?

Dave feels embarrassed for them, and deletes the messages without replying.

At the end of the month, the Managing Director goes into Francesca's office.

'Wait,' Francesca shouts, as the Managing Director closes the door behind him. He lowers the partition blinds, blocking the light from Francesca's window and tilting Dave's desk into the dark. Alan and the other assistants get up, leave their desks, carrying scripts for photocopying and empty mugs to return to the kitchen.

Dave is the only assistant left in the office. She is rescheduling a meeting when she hears Francesca begging in her office.

Dave cannot move until it is over.

When the Managing Director leaves Francesca's office, he passes Dave's desk and tips a pile of paper from Dave's desk onto the floor.

'Clear that up, please, Alan,' he says to Dave.

In her office, Dave helps Francesca up and onto her swivel chair. Francesca's blood is dark as Cabernet. Dave's cardigan makes a cheap tourniquet for her leg; Francesca pulls her own cashmere tightly around herself. When the bleeding stops Dave runs out to buy Francesca new trousers, so that no one sees where Francesca soiled herself. The old carpet was already dirty, but Dave borrows cleaning foam from the dog-room and sprays it thick anyway. She scrubs it hard with a brush; the bristles flick bloodied bubbles of soap and who knows what else into her face.

Perhaps, Dave thinks, I should look for a new dream job.

'Thank you,' Francesca says, from her desk, not meeting Dave's eye, a new draft of a script in front of her. 'I need somewhere nice for dinner. I'm meeting Jeremy Jones.'

The next day Francesca calls Dave into the office and holds both her hands, grinning. Dave is a little afraid.

'Jeremy Jones has signed on,' Francesca says. 'We're going into production.'

Dave thinks of that filthy, smelly metal briefcase and tries not to gag.

'I can't promote you, but you might get a credit,' Francesca says, handing Dave a box. 'I bought you this.'

Dave undoes a delicate noose of ribbon, and folds back gentle layers of tissue paper to find a long, stylish black coat worth at least a month of her rent.

The next few weeks are relaxing. Francesca is away on set. Dave stays quiet in the office. Dave tries not to notice people covering up bruises and cuts; the assistants stay out of each other's business. They fight their own battles with concealer, and beta-blockers, and camomile tea.

Dave is copied into emails with the special effects team discussing the difficulty of editing the suitcase out of scenes in post-production. The other leads complain that the suitcase affects their blocking, and distracts during performance. Wardrobe have to spend time unpicking and resewing Jeremy Jones' left sleeves because he refuses to uncuff it. Dave is constantly scanning clauses of contracts to email through to Francesca.

Going in and out of Francesca's office, Dave becomes aware of how heavy the filing cabinet is when one day a drawer unexpectedly falls from its runners into her hands. The contracts she flicks through are all printed on paper thin as blades. They slit Dave's skin so finely she can barely see it, but she can feel the cuts run deep. When she turns on Francesca's desk lamp, her eyes water.

But then it is awards season.

The company is nominated for everything, and Dave finds it hard not to be grateful for a position at such a winning company. You can't make world-renowned entertainment without getting some paper-cuts, she thinks.

She invites her friends over to watch the ceremony live, but they spend most of the evening catching up among themselves as she strains to hear the results over them.

When the film goes into post-production, Francesca works long hours as the film tips over budget. Jeremy Jones falls out with the director, and the director is now in a different time zone.

Francesca often comes into the office not having been to bed. She spends all night on the phone to one talent, then to another talent. She sits at her desk patting expensive creams under her eyes and drinks so much coffee that Dave can see her hands shake as she types.

Dave wears thicker clothing, more layers. She wraps bandages around her ribs before dressing in the morning, trying to mould an exoskeleton. She tries to spread the impact of Francesca's bad days across her body. She tries to see where it is coming from – the scald of tea, the prick of a drawing pin, the electric shock. She tries not to draw attention to her vulnerability; tries not to let Francesca know it hurts.

Francesca gifts her handbags, jewellery, perfume.

Dave organises an exclusive screening of the finished film. She is given a budget that could be a deposit for a flat in Dave's building. They hold the screening at a five-star hotel over the road, for the rest of the company and other important executives.

Dave lingers at the entrance to the cinema room. The walls

are soundproofed with burgundy leather padding. Dave has a clipboard, although she would never dream of checking a name. The thick-rimmed glasses and sports jackets with jeans all speak for themselves. In the small, stuffy space, the crowd of people make a low grating noise that reminds Dave of a wasp's nest.

Alan passes Dave, holding a glass of white wine. She charges it to Dave, her phantom little finger waving like an invisible flag.

The Managing Director takes the podium and introduces the film. The whole room laughs together at his jokes. If there's one thing you can say about this industry, Dave thinks, it's got a sense of humour.

Dave is listening, learning, so only sees the women rushing past, waving their briefcases, when it is too late.

They rush the stage and push the Managing Director to the floor.

They point down at Jeremy Jones, sitting in the front row, listening to accolades about himself, and scream.

'Give us back our parts.'

'You've deformed us.'

'You're an animal.'

'You're a fucking monster'.

Dave's friends send her messages, worrying about her proximity to Jeremy Jones.

He always seemed perfectly nice, Dave tells them.

The following day Francesca and the Managing Director are shut away in Francesca's office with a crisis management team engaged to protect the film.

By lunchtime Jeremy Jones is arrested at his home. The metal briefcase is unlocked. It contains a multitude of tiny, almost negligible pieces of the human body. Tips of toes, nails, snippets of ear lobe, belly buttons. A little finger. Nothing too obvious. Things that are easily hidden. They have been stored, slopping around together, unpreserved and rotting.

'This is sick,' says Alan, as the news breaks across her screen. Her fork stops, inches from her mouth, above a Tupperware box of grated carrot and vinegar brought in from home. 'I can't read it.' She puts in her mouthguard with her four-fingered hand, before taking her boss his lunch. Poor Alan, Dave thinks, poor, stupid Alan.

When the crisis management meeting is over, Francesca calls Dave into her office, where she sits, scrolling and scrolling through the news.

'Why did they keep working with him?' Dave says, watching over Francesca's shoulder.

'Why did you let them in?' Francesca asks.

How could I have kept them out? Dave thinks as Francesca stands up, takes her by the neck, and slams her face down onto the desk so hard she hears the pen pot jump off the side. For a moment everything goes black and hurts so much that she can't remember whether she is Dave, or someone else entirely.

Dave lies in A&E, thinking of how the rowan tree outside the office – inflamed now with leaves of red, yellow and orange – had shot away from her through the window of the ambulance. When, she thinks, did I last phone home?

She watches the doctors and nurses come and go at the end of her bed. They wear a uniform; they all look the same. Hygienic and pristine. At one point, a group of them all gather around and point at the same clipboard, sharing information, working together. Then they scatter suddenly, spinning away from each other across the smooth, blue, disinfected linoleum. Later, they draw back together again, like magnets.

Dave is checked repeatedly for concussion and receives stitches to her nose. She sees the same doctor over the course of the day. The doctor has to remind herself of Dave's name every time she comes in. She's busy – she apologises each time.

'Just call me Dave.' Dave hears the thickness of her voice through the blocked nose, and is embarrassed for taking up a bed.

The doctor doesn't understand the joke, and doesn't call her Dave, but has to rush away suddenly to an emergency. Dave is not, after all, bleeding to death.

Later, while Dave waits outside to catch the bus home, she touches the stitches on her nose. She presses her bruises gently with her index finger when her phone rings.

'Derek's off sick,' the Managing Director tells her. 'But I want to give you a bonus. Have you got a nice coat?'

'Who's Derek?' Dave asks, but the Managing Director has passed Dave onto his assistant who wants to take Dave's coat size.

Francesca does not come back to work, and does not return Dave's messages. Who, Dave worries, will correct her spelling of 'definately' in emails? Who will assemble her a rainbow power bowl at Vital Salads? Does she even know the phone number for her local non-toxic dry cleaners?

The night of the premiere, Leicester Square's red carpets loll like tongues. Dave's heels pinch and cut into her ankles; it is important to have height in front of cameras.

Dave is relieved that the film screened well despite the adverse publicity. 'It's not just the lead actor, there are so many other people involved in making films,' Dave had told her friends defensively. 'Their hard work deserves a platform too.'

Dave stays in the cinema until the very end to watch the credits roll. Her plush, fold-down seat itches through her low-denier tights.

Sadly, Francesca does not get a credit.

There is a singular, enigmatic name in a column entitled ASSISTANTS.

'Dave'.

It is early. The streets still ghost with fog as Dave walks to the office. Her pockets are filled with absorbent gauze and medical tape. The stitches on her nose have disappeared, like Alan's finger. But Dave wonders if Alan can still feel her phantom digit, the way that Dave can still feel the phantom crack in her face; she wonders whether Alan feels whole and fully herself regardless.

The air is clearer by the time Dave reaches the glass doors. They refract the white sun in awkward constellations. Dave looks at the rowan tree, leafless and bare, to avoid her own reflection as the doors slide slowly apart. She prefers not to see her scar and, instead, her attention is grabbed by the black cabs swinging past, catapulting away to other corners of the city with centrifugal force, ramming themselves up the slim streets, dismissed, as Soho gets to work.

FRIDAY ART CLUB

A LIGHTWEIGHT 1970s hollow core door with a lustrous sapele veneer opens onto a fastidiously clean but spartan back-room office of about three by four metres. The walls are a slightly lighter beige hue than the fitted carpet which was laid thirty years ago but looks brand new. A desk faces away from the door and abuts the far wall below a horizontal slit of a window which is too high to see from. The desk is of a 1980s middle manager style, dark wood veneer on a black plastic-coated box steel frame. The only thing on its surface is an old BT cordless phone, the cables from which hang down the wall to a socket mounted just above the skirting. The only other object in the room is the dark grey polycotton upholstered swivel chair.

Through another sapele doorway sits Mr Weatherburn at a round dark wood dining table with turned spindle legs. He wears a red V-neck golfing sweater and a pair of grey flat front trousers in a low-maintenance wool blend. He has a newspaper spread out on the table.

On the radio a famous entrepreneurial disruptor is attempting to validate his business model. He explains how he is disrupting the corporate establishment by using the same techniques that the corporate establishment used to disrupt the corporate establishment that preceded it and which are, in all probability, the same techniques that the corporate establishment before that used to disrupt the corporate establishment that preceded that too. Mr Weatherburn isn't really listening anymore.

Mr Weatherburn closes the paper. Underneath it is a copy of *Britain Yesterday and Today* with a foreword by Peter Sissons which he briefly flicks through before getting to his feet. He wanders into the kitchen, switches off the radio and rinses a mug while he gazes out of the window. In the field at the back he can see a young woman in denim shorts and a vest top cutting down the ragwort with a scythe. He decides to take the dog out for a walk.

Mr Weatherburn takes off his slippers by the front door and then ties the laces of his Clark's Natures, resting each foot in turn on the Saxony-cut carpet of the staircase. He fumbles for a dog lead under the navy-blue anorak that hangs from the hooks in the hallway, the sound of which brings Max the labrador out from the front room.

Mr Weatherburn and Max wander up the unmade track between the thorns and brambles past regular mounds of cut thistle and ragwort. It's warm and the ground is hard. Butterflies flit around the buddleia. The thrum of an approaching vehicle grows steadily louder until birds scatter from the undergrowth and Mr Weatherburn and Max are briefly forced over into the spongy tussock grass at the edge of the path. A group of men in period costume bounce by in a small Mercedes bus on their way to re-enact the Battle of Wakefield in the top field again. Mr Weatherburn holds on to the top stones of the wall for balance on the uneven ground.

Mr Weatherburn continues on his way and as the track

widens at the entrance to the community farm, he stops to talk to Mr Davies from the barn conversion on the ridge. They discuss their experiences of electrocardiography –

'It makes your arm twitch, doesn't it?'

and their problems with spam emails –

'I pressed something on the moving around thing on the screen, not the mouse, the other thing, and I put it on something else and now I keep getting emails from people in Bradford asking if I can come and help move some furniture for them.'

Max dashes through the heather with Mr Davies's springer spaniel, Jill. Eventually Mr Davies says he has to get off because her indoors will be wondering what he's up to.

Mr Weatherburn takes the old cart track up towards the road that circumnavigates the hill with the best views. At the top he hitches Max to the footpath sign and turns to look across the town below while he catches his breath. The chapel, the school, the pub, the engineering works, everything: apple bobbing, Cliff's jumper and the bright orange wax in his ear, Mrs Allen's Wood's Ware and the musty wainscoting, muffled hymns, heavy coats and misty playgrounds, Kicky Hinchliffe, the Ford Anglia, the Hillman Hunter, Dad falling off the ladder at Joe's, Pam on Thursdays in town, working on the DB5 chassis platforms, the office with Brian, Dennis's stories in the canteen, Pam's mum that Christmas, watching Chris play football in the rain, singing Sinatra on the school run with Sarah, the weddings, Danny's first time at the pictures . . .

The postman pulls up in the squeaky red Peugeot Partner with part of the bumper fastened on with cable ties.

'Mr Weatherburn, I'm glad I've caught you. I've got a parcel for you.' The postman hands over a package. 'Too big to go through the box.'

'Thanks, lad,' says Mr Weatherburn. 'Much left to do?'

'No, thank God. I've had enough of delivering meerkats and sex toys for one day,' says the postman with a pantomime grin and two fingers to his temple like a gun.

Mr Weatherburn sets off again. He climbs the stone stile and joins the narrow footpath across the tussock moor where he lets Max off his lead. A man with a swagger and a grey hoody makes his way in the opposite direction. His dog, a black and tan Jack Russell terrier, catches sight of Max and runs towards him barking aggressively. Max stands his ground, the hair down his back on end. The terrier moves in again but Max fends him off. The stand-off continues and the man in the hoody is running now.

'PEANUT!' he yells, 'Peanut!' again, 'Peanut!'

By the second 'Peanut' his conviction is on the wane and by the third it is all but smothered by his obvious embarrassment at the dog's name.

'It's okay,' shouts Mr Weatherburn. 'No harm done. And, by the way, Peanut is a perfectly good name for a black and tan Jack Russell. Let's shout it together. PEEAANNUTT!" yells Mr Weatherburn at the top of his voice. Peanut and Max look up.

'And again,' shouts Mr Weatherburn.

"PEANUT!" Both men shout together. Peanut looks quizzical, head cocked. Both men laugh.

'Come on, Peanut!' shouts the hoody man again and Peanut runs towards him.

Mr Weatherburn and Max set off down the road in the direction of the shops and Mr Weatherburn can't help smiling as they pass two chubby men in puffer jackets who are having a loud discussion about how much of a dick one of their acquaintances is. The man in the beige jacket says he's 'a right dick' and the man in the blue jacket says he's 'a total dick'.

Mr Weatherburn ties Max to the railings outside the Co-op and goes inside. He ambles along the aisles accompanied by the greatest hits of the 1970s and 80s: 'Let's Groove', Earth Wind & Fire; 'China in Your Hands', T'Pau; 'Have You Seen Her?' The Chi-Lites. He is briefly confused by the newly installed chiller cabinets; the doors open the opposite way to the old ones and he grabs for a non-existent handle. The girl with the glittery make-up points out the problem. She says she did exactly the same thing herself.

In the queue at the checkout, the man in front of Mr Weatherburn is wearing pyjamas and the man behind is humming along to '(I Just) Died In Your Arms Tonight' by Cutting Crew.

'Pop your PIN in, buddy,' says the young man with the bum-fluff beard while Mr Weatherburn is concentrating on not crushing his fish fingers with his potatoes.

On his way out of the shop, Mr Weatherburn pauses at the charity book sale table and puts 50p in the box for the hardback copy of Alec Waugh's *Island in the Sun*, then he scans the small ads on the index cards which are stuck to a cork board with drawing pins. Among the handwritten offers of childcare and gardening services there's 'Two female life models required £10.00/hour'. To Mr Weatherburn's amusement the contact phone number is only one digit away from his own. He stifles a laugh; he now has an explanation for the strange phone call he received last weekend. He considers this would make an excellent anecdote and he looks around the shop for somebody to tell. He glances back over to the charity book table where the big man with the tattooed neck is leafing through a biography of Donald Wolfit. Mr Weatherburn decides he isn't confident the tattooed neck man would make a very receptive audience; one teatime, a couple of years ago, he had to pull him out of the road where he'd fallen asleep with a half-eaten bag of sweet chilli crisps splayed open on his stomach. In the end Mr Weatherburn decides to leave the shop without mentioning the phone number thing. Perhaps he can tell Sarah about it the next time she rings.

Mr Weatherburn unhitches Max from the railings and they make their way back home the road way. They pass the man walking laps of his small front yard, his arms behind his back and his gaze steadfastly fixed on the middle distance. They pass the offices of the suppliers of aseptic isolation systems, a sign displayed prominently in the window: ON FRIDAYS OUR STAFF HAVE THE RIGHT TO DRESS DOWN. On they go, past the headless pigeon on the pavement outside the newsagent's shop, past the tall man with the wire-rimmed specs who is listening to Bob Marley on speaker-phone, past the closed-down shop with the faded sign: HALAL MEAT OFF-LICENCE. They make their way onto the top road where the pavement is adjoined by a high wall for its entire length. Mr Weatherburn finds himself overcome with curiosity. What is on the other side of that wall? He must have walked down this street a thousand times and has never thought to find out. He looks down the length of it to see whether there's a lower section he might be able to glimpse over but the wall continues unbroken at its regular height, half a metre above Mr Weatherburn's head. Fifty metres in the distance, just after the big junction box, two large gateposts mark what must have, at one time, been an entrance, but the space between them has been bricked up for as long as Mr Weatherburn can remember. He turns to look back the way he's come and, twenty metres back just after the shop, in amongst the dock leaves and nettles, a fire hydrant marker on a foot-high concrete post abuts the base of the wall. Mr Weatherburn pulls Max round and they make their way over. He drops the bag of shopping and Max's lead. 'Stay there, lad,' he says, and he steps up onto the marker with his right foot. From here he grasps the top of the triangular coping with both hands, wedges the sole of his left shoe into the roughly finished stone of the wall and pulls himself up another half metre or so, his hands shaking with the exertion of maintaining a grip. Then he transfers enough of his weight onto his left foot for just long enough to let go of the coping with his right hand. He swings his elbow over the top, grazing his forearm in the process. He hangs there for a moment while he aligns his varifocals to accurately assess the damage. There's blood, but not too much. Now he heaves his other elbow over, braces both forearms against the far side of the coping and pulls his head and chest above the top of the wall. Both his feet dance around for cracks to settle in. And there, stretching away from him is an unkempt area of broken asphalt, couch grass, brambles and sycamore saplings which Mr Weatherburn recognises as part of the grounds of the hospital that closed down over a decade ago now. 'Probably the old car park,' he says to himself and he slides down from the wall and dabs at his blooded arm with a pocket handkerchief, it's not as bad as it looks. He picks up his shopping and Max's lead and continues on his way home.

Mr Weatherburn opens the door and unhooks Max who

saunters into the front room and flops down in his usual place by the weeping fig. Mr Weatherburn takes off his shoes and then climbs the stairs to the bathroom where he bathes his arm with warm water and TCP. In the kitchen he boils the kettle for a cup of tea and opens a tin of sardines from the Co-op bag. He sits at the table and eats them with a squirt of lemon juice while flicking through *Britain Yesterday and Today*.

Mr Weatherburn spends the afternoon chopping hard-boiled eggs to make sandwiches, his contribution to the Lonely Arts Club artists' annual event at the village hall which marks the culmination of a weekend of open studios in the town. This is the sixteenth year that Mr Weatherburn has been involved in some capacity. His wife, Pam, had been an accomplished water colourist and he had initially volunteered to show his support of her. He'd help out hanging pictures, building displays and sometimes issuing raffle tickets at the door. As the years had gone by he'd found he got along well with the 'arty set'. He enjoyed seeing people expressing their creativity. He became more and more involved until he'd found himself chair of the hanging committee.

While Mr Weatherburn was well liked, his promotion to what was in effect the most senior curatorial role in the organisation was seen in some quarters as controversial on account of his lack of any real creative experience. On one memorable occasion, Mr Weatherburn had been embarrassed when he was harangued at a preview evening by Russell Lockwood, one of the artists from the studios in the repurposed old mill. Mr Lockwood had been very unhappy with the hang. He'd also been very drunk and, in Mr Weatherburn's view, extremely rude. In response Mr Weatherburn had maintained his propriety and had simply and calmly explained to Mr Lockwood that his only motivation for accepting the role was his desire to help. The role had needed filling, nobody had put themselves forward and so he'd stepped in. Mr Lockwood had stormed out nevertheless, deliberately smashing Mrs Geldart's stained glass sculpture of a pair of butterflies in the process, an act which earned him a lifetime ban.

Even though most of those gathered had been quick to show their support for Mr Weatherburn, including the other mill artists and certainly the rest of the committee, Pam had seen fit to procure him a generous measure of Scotch to calm his nerves. The whole debacle had unnerved him greatly. He was, and remains to this day, very confused by it.

Ever since Pam died, Mr Weatherburn has preferred to take more of a back seat as far as the annual artists' event is concerned but when called upon he will always make himself available. He recognises how much the arty set did for his wife's confidence and well-being through some difficult times.

At 5pm the landline rings in the office.

'Hello, is that Mr Weatherburn? It's Verity, Mrs Wilkinson, from Art Club. I'm sorry about this, I hope it's not too late, but could you perhaps do cheese sandwiches instead of egg? We're going to have to manage without egg this year with all the concerns about allergies . . . Better to be safe than sorry.'

Mr Weatherburn replaces the handset into its cradle, collects his keys and wallet and reverses the Skoda from the drive. He might just make it back to the Co-op for before it shuts.

Mr Weatherburn returns home with bread, butter, cheese, pickle and a ready-meal shepherd's pie for one which he puts in the oven before he gets started. Next, he sets about grating a small mountain of cheese while he half listens to a radio play about Eleanor of Aquitaine. When the pie is cooked, he breaks off for an hour to eat it in front of the television with Max. He catches the second half of the England game while Max lies on his feet.

After the game, a draw, Mr Weatherburn constructs the sandwiches, plates them up under clingfilm and carefully stacks them in the fridge, then he lets Max out into the garden while he washes up and tidies round. He picks up the Co-op bag and realises that he's left the parcel that the postman gave him inside it. He tears open the outer layer of brown paper. Underneath is a belated birthday card and a present from Sarah. *Dad, sorry it's a bit late but I think you'll agree it was worth waiting for x.*

Mr Weatherburn opens the next layer of wrapping paper and finds an original 1:24 1965 Airfix kit of an Aston Martin DB5. 'Wow,' he says to himself as he inspects the artwork on the box. James Bond is dispatching another villain via the car's famous ejector seat.

Mr Weatherburn warms some milk on the hob, fetches Max back inside and makes his way up to bed with his bedtime whisky and his birthday present. The weekend starts now.

KAMILA SHAMSIE

CHURAIL

MY FATHER MIGRATED to England with me weeks after I was born to protect us from my mother, who had died giving birth to me. My cousin, Zainab, informed me of my starring role in this turn of events when I was six years old and my father was preparing to move us to London from Manchester, where we'd been living with Zainab's parents. It's important to hear the truth, Zainab told me, with the solemnity of an eleven-year-old who doesn't know when she might ever again see her young cousin. There were four miscarriages before I came along, and after the second the doctors advised against further pregnancies. My mother talked of adoption, but my father was insistent that he must have a son of his own blood, and the universe responded as it does when men refuse to understand what nature is trying to tell them: it gave him the wrong kind of child, and it took away his wife.

It was summer. We were sitting on the floor of Zainab's bedroom, which she'd consented to share with me since I was old enough to be moved out of the crib next to my aunt's bedside. Serena Williams and One Direction looked down at us as the July rain blurred the world outside in its predictable way. Zainab took my hand in hers. The next bit was the most important, she said.

I was only days old when my father heard a woman's voice calling his name from the peepul tree that grew across the street from our home. He looked up at the first call, strode to the door at the second, and was bloodless with terror, immobilised, when no third call came. My wet-nurse saw it all, and she was the one to spread it through our village that my mother had become a churail.

Women who died in childbirth often became churail, and were known for their fondness for living in peepul trees and calling out to their victims in the sweetest of voices. A misty dark night was the most dangerous time to be enticed by a churail because you might see only the beauty of her face and miss the telltale sign of feet turned backwards at the ankle. The other clue to the churail was that she would always call her victim's name twice – never once, never three times. She would lure men to her hiding place and keep them there, draining them of their life force, until they were old and spent. When she released them back into the world they'd find decades had gone by and everyone they knew was dead, so they would end their lives alone and unloved.

Basically, Rip van Winkle is the story of a man spirited away by a churail but with the sex censored, Zainab said, briefly her usual self, trying to throw the word 'sex' in my direction at any opportunity just to see me squirm. Then she turned serious again: When your father says he'll never go back to Pakistan because it's a terrible place, don't believe him. He won't go back because he's afraid the churail is waiting for him.

We moved from Manchester to London when I was six, from Wembley to Queen's Park when I was eight, and from Queen's

Park to Kensington when I was nine. With the move from one Kensington property to the next, my father's life finally caught up with his ambitions when I was twelve. He bought a house with a garden – the seventh largest in London, six places down from Buckingham Palace – and said we would never move again. You can make friends now, he said, as though it were the change in addresses rather than the awkwardness and insecurity of my character that had impeded my social life. He sent me to the most expensive school he could find and told me not to mix with the wrong kind of girl, by which I knew he meant other Pakistanis. He had huge disdain for his brother who had moved to England without any interest in becoming English – if you enter someone's home as a guest you must find ways of being pleasing to them, he liked to say. His way of being pleasing to the English was to take up squash, hire an accent coach, become a donor to the arts and a member of a venerable men-only club. But his attempts to showcase me as the perfect immigrant daughter resulted in disappointment: the piano teacher, the tennis coach, the French au pairs left only the faintest impression, quickly smudged.

One day he came home to find me in the kitchen, and although I wasn't doing anything other than bending down to the vegetable drawer in our fridge on my way to assembling a sandwich the sight of me made him cry out in rage.

No matter what I do you'll always look like a peasant working in the fields, he said.

And then a miracle occurred. When I was sixteen, Zainab moved to London for an investment banking job after a glittering turn at university. She was everything my father wanted me to be: stylish, skilled in small-talk, ambitious, opening bat for the City Ladies Cricket Club. He encouraged her to treat our home as though it were hers, seemed pleased whenever he saw her walk through the front door, laughed at her jokes, asked about her life. I couldn't hate her for it, and she quickly took up her old position as the shining centre of my life. In return, she appeared to find genuine pleasure in my company, which made me relax and talk openly with her in a way I never did with anyone else.

Her reappearance brought back an old memory, and one afternoon I asked her about the churail.

She typed something into her phone as we reclined on adjoining garden chairs under the umbrella on an unnaturally hot autumn day.

Listen! These are all the circumstances under which a woman can become a churail.

Dying in childbirth, that was the first. Also, dying during pregnancy.

Dying during the period of lying-in (we had to look up 'lying-in', which didn't mean a lazy Sunday morning). Dying in bed.

Dying while on your period. Dying in any unnatural or tragic way. Dying after a life during which the woman has experienced abuse at the hands of a man. Dying after a life during which the woman has experienced abuse at the hands of her in-laws. Dying after a life of little or no sexual fulfilment.

Well! Zainab said.

Soon we were shouting out names of dead women who were clearly now churail: Marilyn Monroe (died in bed); Zainab's one-time neighbour Aunty Rubina (no sexual fulfil- ment, obviously); Amy Winehouse (unnatural death); Carrie

Fisher (tragic death, because no matter how Princess Leia dies it's tragic); Princess Diana (in-laws).

Later that day, my father asked what Zainab and I had been laughing about so hysterically he had to close the windows to his study. He was on his way out when he said that, front-door keys in his hand, and I knew the remark was a rebuke phrased as a question but even so I chose to answer it:

Churail.

He slipped the keys into his pocket, but not before I heard them jangle in his usually steady hand.

Superstitious nonsense, he said, and departed, leaving me alone. We had dispensed with au pairs when I turned thirteen, and instead he had cameras all over the house, presumably so he could replay the footage of any disaster that might kill or maim or assault me while he was out. This was the sort of thing I thought often and never said out loud, except to Zainab.

The next day Zainab texted to say my father had banned her from seeing me any more. When I went weeping to my father, he said, Exactly the kind of bad influence I've tried my whole life to keep you away from.

A tiny part of me was relieved that I wouldn't have to watch him around Zainab and know he wasn't incapable of love, just that he was incapable of loving me.

My father's version of our migration story was this: when my mother died, my uncle called from Manchester and said his business was expanding, he could do with my father's help and my aunt would raise me with Zainab as my older sister. And so my father came to England, mostly for my sake. It was only once he'd arrived that he saw two things: (a) the country he had left was a dump to which he intended never to return, and (b) he could become a rich man here, but not while attached to his brother's mini-cab company. There were several failed ventures before he made his first million from a marriage app targeting a Muslim clientele ('Discounts on venue hire, catering, car service and outfit tailoring for all our satisfied customers!').

Why didn't you ever marry again? I asked when I could speak to him once more. Didn't you want a son? Sometimes there were short-term girlfriends in his life, but I was certain that most of his relations with women were uncomplicatedly transactional.

Not once I understood there are other ways to leave a legacy, he said. He was a man who liked to stamp his name on things - university scholarships, renovated theatre foyers, museum wings.

And what am I? I said.

He switched on the TV and turned his attention to *Dancing with the Stars*.

I continued to see Zainab, but furtively. She didn't set foot in our house again until the following summer when she entered no further than the hallway, front door open behind her, and asked me to let my father know she would like to talk to him.

It was the summer of floods in Pakistan, devastation without precedent. Zainab had quit her investment banking job, and was on her way to Pakistan to help with flood relief. She told my father she had come to see him, hat in hand (she was wearing a fedora, which she doffed in his direction as she spoke), to ask for a donation to the aid organisation she would be working with. His village was underwater, she said.

My village is Kensington and Chelsea, he said, and turned on his heels, still nimble in his movements despite his increased girth.

Your family has lost everything, she called out. Your uncles, your cousins.

He didn't falter as he continued down the hall to his study, and I remembered the only time I had seen his body betray the tiniest disruption to his psyche.

I walked Zainab down the street to the nearest cash machine so I could withdraw the maximum amount my debit card allowed, and our conversation returned to the churail, who had led first to my exile from Pakistan, then Zainab's expulsion from my home.

She's the victim of patriarchy who enacts revenge on men, I said. I guess that's kind of feminist?

Except she's evil, Zainab said. And she's evil because she's attractive and without sexual restraint.

She's a manifestation of patriarchy's guilt, I said.

She allows guilty men to cast themselves as the victims, Zainab said.

And even when they're the victims they make themselves sex-gods with a fifty-year-long erection that a woman of unearthly beauty can't get enough of.

Zainab laughed and laughed.

Be this version of yourself more, she said.

Seriously, there are no queer churail?

Yes, like that, like that.

≈

I told Zainab that when I turned eighteen I would go to our family's village and visit my mother's grave. But when she returned from Pakistan it was with the news that the graveyard had been washed away in the flooding, along with every home in the village. Even the peepul tree, she said, even that had been destroyed. She placed a green-brown section of branch in my hand, six or seven inches long, with small heart-shaped leaves growing from it. This was the only thing I could bring back for you, she said. Think of it as a climate refugee.

A climate refugee in a hostile environment, I said, knowing that peepul trees can't grow in England. They want sun and humidity to thrive. Even so, I planted the cutting in the corner of our garden where there was the most sunlight. It was still summer in England, and hotter than any summer before. In the next weeks it grew a few centimetres, and then autumn came, and winter after, and though the peepul tree didn't die it stagnated, a stubby sad thing that the gardener wanted to uproot until our cook from Sri Lanka told him it had religious significance. My father was unaware of this piece of his village growing in the English garden he treated as entirely ornamental for visitors to look at admiringly from the windows of the house.

The following year, the summer heat came earlier, more ferociously. By June we already had hosepipe bans in London and the grass in the garden was burnt, the trees wilted. One weekend morning only a trickle of water came from the kitchen tap. We thought at first it was the drought, but every other tap gushed water. My father said he would call a plumber and I thought no more of it until I heard my father roaring my name from a corner of the garden I hadn't walked to in months.

The peepul was five or so feet high, its heart-shaped leaves thick and glossy. The plumber had his phone in his hand, one of those apps open that identifies plants. He called it 'invasive'; he said it could send its roots deep and far in search of water. It had entered our pipes, might already be burrowing its way into the foundation of the house.

How is this here? my father said.

I told him Zainab had brought it, clipped from the peepul tree across the street from our house.

His face! Like a man receiving news of a sickness so old and deep in him that there's no way of cutting it out without excising his organs with it.

The plumber, reading off the screen, said we would have to call in an expert to remove it. Cut down the plant and the roots would continue to grow. Hard to know what damage had already been done.

That night my father stood in the rarely used drawing room, looking out at the seventh largest garden in London. We'd been leaving the windows open at night to let in the breeze but as I walked through the house in search of him I saw that each one was closed and locked. I went to stand beside him.

Do you see her? he said.

It was a spindly little thing, with nothing of the magnificence of the broad-trunked peepul I'd seen in pictures, with their aerial roots, their great height. We stood there a long time, the only sound his breath, strange and ragged. He didn't seem aware of my presence, appeared not to notice that I hadn't answered his question. The moon slid out from cloud;

the breeze stirred the branches and leaves. I saw a slender-limbed figure hold out her arms towards the house. I heard a voice say a name, twice.

My name.

My father looked at me.

Very calmly, as if I had been waiting for this all my life, I walked towards the French windows and unbolted them. My father's hand clamped onto my wrist.

She won't like it if you do that, I said, and he moved his hand away as though my skin were poison.

I stepped into the garden. Dead grass beneath my bare feet. Across the burnt expanse the tree waited. Perhaps I would find my cousin Zainab hiding in the darkness. Perhaps I would find the real truth of the churail, a creature much older than the myths men wove around her, desperate to be the centre of her story.

One step and then another and another. I stopped, sat on the grass, and hugged my legs to my chest, my face turned up to the sky. There was no rush. I would sit there awhile, and my father would stand and watch me while the echo of the churail's voice burrowed deep inside him, shaking every foundation.

NICHOLAS ROYLE

STRANGERS MEET
WE WHEN

THERE WAS THE room where the painter slept and kept her things and on a gorgeous sunny spring day only just introduced themselves to one another when her big sister Effie called up needing help with something downstairs and it wasn't supposed to take five minutes the younger had said fearing it might be twenty and flustered but trusting she'd made her apologies and would be back.

It was the dog had something stuck in his paw or cut it poor thing but she didn't want to explain because this was not a vet's surgery nor a day for Effie to be part of but the hour for showing the picture and settling the commission and the tea would stay hot under the cosy and Miss Blyton had said right out she'd something to read and was happy with her nose in it for as long as the painter needed.

No one to know her undermind the author closed her eyes.

Such a glorious morning and that girl so funny and full of go with her Dublin accent disappearing into English reminded her of her grandmother and what a lovely room with the fresh flowers in jugs in practically every corner and the warm sun stirring the Queen of the Suburbs out of the windows distant sounds of omnibus and car and carriage away across the park with all the trees coming into blossom and the birds singing as if the world was on fire in the gathering heat of the morning.

There was the painter's easel with her latest work taking form and the newcomer might feign not to have noticed the splendour of its quietness a watercolour of a great tree she hadn't yet decided still its beauty gave her a queer sense of having seen it before.

For equally she might in these minutes have brazenly fingered the portfolio by the little bed doubtless placed conveniently for its owner to unfasten the little black ribbons and display but this she saw was a feat too far for the exacting bows and retying without notice and anyway that might spoil a pleasure.

But a roving eye was hers and she was hardly going to nestle in these cushions beside the tea-tray and bowl of something freshly baked under a neat starched tea-towel reading as if under obligation the book she'd brought with her for why would you do that when you're suddenly alone in a lovely stranger's room without the stranger.

Unless it was a book belonging to the stranger was how she saw it and it fell out when treading softly alert as a thief to a creaking board she dipped her face towards the narcissi on the table keen for the fragrance of their stems as much as flowers and skirting the pretty spray of cherry blossom in the fireplace after checking herself in the mirror over the mantelpiece to see the new red dress just right with the pearls.

Miss Blyton scanned the shelf skipping novels by Scott and

Dickens and Henty and Wells and the poems of Yeats and de la Mare and Brooke and Drinkwater her eyes alighting on a slender black spine of more anonymous and lowly origins and how pleased she felt with this speed and felicity a gift she possessed like her powers of memory only glance at a page and have it by heart.

And so she slid out and proceeded to read knowing she shouldn't the Paris and Swiss Journal of Lola Onslow dated May 26th 1911 occupying the first forty pages of an otherwise blank notebook.

We started off on <u>*Monday April 24th 1911*</u> *by the 6.15 train from West Ealing station to Victoria. A friend of ours, Irene Harman & Nellie, our cook saw us off. We were very excited. When we arrived at Victoria we had nearly an hour to wait, so Effie & I amused ourselves by exploring the station. When the train came in we secured our seats, & settled down for the journey to Newhaven. The train started at 8.45. A young friend of Miss Bazett's, Winnie Binning, was coming with us as far as Lausanne, where she was going to teach at a school. Effie & Winnie did not sleep at all during the journey to Newhaven, but I slept a little. We arrived at Newhaven at about 10.30. Our luggage had been [put, she must have meant] through to Paris, & so we had nothing to do with it, until we reached Paris. We went on board the SS Brighton, & went down into our cabin, there were two rows of berths round it. So Effie & I each secured a top one. We were given rugs to cover us with, by the stewardess, who was very nice. When the boat started, she turned down the lights. Beside our births there were*

*portholes, & Effie & I spent most of our time, looking
out through them, at the waves.*

O how powerfully in waves it brought back the excitement
of her own first journey abroad with her beloved Louise to
Annecy just two years later never to be forgotten.

It was bad form but awfully pleasing to read someone else's
journal and a good reason she herself kept no record of what
most mattered never to reveal the intimacies and intricacies
of her rages and longings concerning her father and mother
and brothers not to mention heady ambitions for writing and
desires for other girls.

It was childlikeness before any betrayal made her a good
Froebel teacher and now governess and what always out-
stripped in gaiety and innocence any respect for the world of
the grown up for wasn't being a grown up the biggest betrayal
of all wasn't de la Mare right when he said what was it he
said 'children are butterflies' who most of them 'by a curious
inversion of the processes of nature become half-comatose and
purblind chrysalides'.

O to be off on an adventure with a sister how she always
longed for a sister all at sea with her gazing through portholes.

Conscience and anticipation tingling she turned the pages
absorbing the pleasure of this girl's continentalising and while
poised at a second's notice for the door was ajar and she must
certainly catch Miss Onslow's steps coming back up the stair
to shut and replace the journal and appear merely to be sur-
veying the volumes on the shelf she was unable to stop.

The prudent thing it occurred to her was to have an alibi
volume to hand not merely gormless at the shelf and so she
picked out *The Wilde Swans at Coole* setting it open on the

book tops and returned to what she shouldn't have been doing.

She revelled in the girl's hand with its looping elegance and charming Q's and V's and I's and B's and ampersands and all her precision with the times of trains departing and arriving and the trees on the way from Dieppe with *large quantities of mistletoe* and the rain *coming down in torrents* and then the sun and churches in Paris and breakfast and dinner and supper and the *rolls and chocolate* and *drink of milk* in a café and lemonade for refreshment and the little steamer down the Seine and the Flower Market at La Sainte Chapelle and the museum with the candid admiration surely an interesting sign of the paintings of Rosa Bonheur at the Palais de Luxembourg *once an old palace but now a picture gallery* with all the little trips around the city by carriage and then the girl's *first ever journey in a taxi* making for the Gare de Lyon they *went whizzing along so quickly* seeing Paris by night *all lit up* before the train out of France.

Miss Blyton's fingers took her eyes to Switzerland.

<u>Tuesday</u> May 2nd. In the morning we walked up to the Signal, to see a lovely view of the lake & mountains. When we got to the top we sat down & Miss Isa read to us. Then we came home, on the way we picked, cowslips, anemones, violets, cuckoo pint, primroses, primulas, and ranunculus. In the afternoon we had two Finland ladies to tea, & afterwards we went for a walk with them. Miss Isa & they sat down on a little hill, & Miss Bazett, Effie & I did a little exploring. We went through a dear little wood, where we saw enormous snails, which, Miss Bazett says, are eaten for consumption. Beyond the wood was

*a field &, in it we found our first small blue gentians.
Afterwards we went home to supper, & bed.*

    <u>Wednesday</u>. *In the morning we walked to the village
& back: and in the afternoon, went for a walk through
some fields to look for some more gentians. A lady had
told us of a place where she had found some. When we had
passed a wood we had to go through first, and come to the
field beyond, great was our surprise to find that it was the
same place we had gone to the day before.*

    <u>Thursday</u>. *After breakfast we walked to 'Lake Bret'.
It was a very pretty walk. We came home in time for
dinner. After dinner we made friends with a little French
girl whose grandmother was stay [staying, of course] at
our Pension. Her name is Jeanne, & she had come over
with her mother, with the purpose of going to Vevey, but
instead she came with us for a walk, while her mother
& grandmother went to Vevey. So we took some oranges
& things, & set off for Lake Bret. We took with us some
mountain sticks we had just bought in the village before
we came out. We played by the lake for some time, &
then sat down & had some refreshments. Jeanne fed a
big snail with orange & it eat [or ate: a mistake I make
too!] a lot of it. After we had finished we went for a
little walk by the side of the lake, & then came home.
Before supper, we played hide & seek, & after supper,
patiences. At about 8.30 Jeanne had to go home. When
she had gone Effie & I went to bed.*

The visitor was streaming through the final entries when the
step of her subject now thirteen years older sounded on the
stair and she scrambled to stow the journal and picked up

the Yeats and in her revery having practically forgotten what Lola looked like felt a fresh flush of pleasure at the pale linen simplicity of her dress and bare feet and glad grace the pretty face and winning smile mingled with the triumph of concealment accomplished.

Less to cap the profusion of apologies and confirmation that the dog was fine than to close the chapter of her clandestine activity she recited as if by heart the start of the poem on the page she had happened to leave open.

> May God be praised for woman
> That gives up all her mind,
> A man may find in no man
> A friendship of her kind
> That covers all he has brought
> As with her flesh and bone,
> Nor quarrels with a thought
> Because it is not her own.

Miss Blyton visibly coloured at the irony and smiled and gave the title 'On Woman' before asking would Lola if she didn't mind first names would Lola like to show the picture now or sit and have tea and the painter tickled to be addressed as Lola but unsure at this momentary reversal of roles said tea when in truth she would have preferred settling the picture.

So they sat on the floor and drank tea still hot and Lola sliced lemon cake still flustered to think Miss Blyton no Enid really was so much the author already found herself divulging as she otherwise very well might not have done that *her* mother was an author too.

Enid looked at Lola and thought of the tomb of Captain

Arkwright *who was lost in an avalanche on Mont Blanc and his body was not found until 31 years afterwards when it was discovered in the stream that runs underneath the glacier.*

That passage had frozen in her mind and she saw it as clearly as she saw the girl.

Said Lola:

- My mother is an author and she's published a book you won't know I'm sure.

At which the painter rose almost spilling her tea veering across the room to gather from a small shelf by the bed her mother's *Faces and How to Read Them.*

- It was published just recently.

And passing the book to the visitor she rushed to fill the space saying

- She publishes as Irma Blood but her real name is Katherine and my sister Effie says sometimes she's away with the fairies.

Which made Enid laugh and also Lola but for a moment more awkwardly.

- Mother thinks you can judge someone's character by the shape and size of their mouth or nose or the distance between their eyes and Effie says Mother is entitled to her opinions but Mother says she received the gift.

Truly there was something about this painter's elfin looks and lilt of voice and half swallowing words with her shyness but the author remarked only

- Delicious cake!

which Lola ignored as she was trying to explain:

- Her father worked on the railways in India when Mother was a girl and she was an only child in a vast foreign place left during the day to wander by herself and one morning she heard strange noises on the other side of the compound wall down among the trees and peered over to see a very old man simply lying by the roadside and she must have communicated with him but it can't have been in English as he wouldn't have spoken that language but it was hot already and he was resting against the wall in the shade of the trees.

Then the Indian Irish English girl as Enid was now thinking paused as if to let her own words catch up with her before carrying on.

– Mother must have been only so high herself.

And Lola raised a slender lovely bare arm again almost but not spilling her tea in the process.

– But she felt such pity for this wizened little fellow by the road I suppose one didn't need to speak the same language to know a body was hungry and she came to learn he was there every day propped up by the roadside in the shade of the tamarind trees and she carried a bowl of gruel to him each morning for breakfast because he had no teeth he was so old Mother said his bones had turned to jelly and later in the day friends would come and bear him to the marketplace and tie them in knots and when Mother had to leave India and return to Ireland on the final morning she took him his gruel and the old man my Mother says passed on to her the gift.

– Of tying people's limbs in knots? interposed Enid laughing.

– No not that at all but Mother's gift as a witch.

Then the visitor opened the book and half-inclined to giggle but maintaining a serious expression read off from the inside board the advertisements for other *Useful Handbooks on Character Reading and Fortune Telling.*

– *Hands and How to Read Them . . . Heads and How to*

Read Them . . . After-Dinner Sleights and Pocket Tricks . . .
Card Tricks Without Sleight of Hand or Apparatus . . . Simple
Conjuring Tricks that Anybody can Perform . . . Hand Shadows:
The Complete Art of Shadowgraphy . . .

- *Shadowgraphy* repeated the visitor at the end and they
both laughed because Enid without meaning for a moment
to do so had pronounced this word with an Irish accent as
if she were Lola or her own grandmother Mary Ann Hanly
now.

Then the visitor turned a couple of pages and delivered
in a voice at once sympathetic and playful words Lola well
recognised.

- *There is something very fascinating about the study of*
faces; we can learn so much from the observation of our fellow-
creatures. It is a useful study, too; so useful that it would be a
wise thing for everyone to gain a slight knowledge, if no more,
as a guide to the placing of trustworthy persons, or the reverse,
either in our affections or in our business concerns.

The young women both orphans of a sort regarded one
another with laughing eyes and Lola hardly knew but as Enid
passed the book back their hands touched in a mild but thrill-
ing instant and enquired as if no one had ever posed such a
question before

- Shall you show me your picture?

Which gave rise to a quite other giddiness for the painting
Lola showed struck Enid as vivid with a delicacy and intricacy
akin to Brueghel's *Landscape with the Fall of Icarus* a heavily
turreted sunlit fairy castle occupying an island all of its own
in the manner of Mont St Michel but with a dreamy bridge
to a nearby land and magically impossibly tall-looking trees
at whose roots beautiful young fairy women gazed at the

approach of goblins and a great old ship set sail for the deep blue horizon.

She was in love with it without a word.

– You've always painted?

This was all Enid could say even though she knew already because the girl writing in her 1911 journal kept referring to the fact that she was painting and drawing and other images now flashed through her mind of Lola's picking *periwinkles and narcissi* and going to the post office to send *boxes of flowers back to England* and the *spray of white lilac* in the Swiss hotel foyer *for the wedding* and then she asked to see other pictures but hardly had to glance at a couple of these marvels of the Little People to wonder would Lola consider also painting a frontispiece for her work was so lovely and the author's heart was pounding so funnily in her chest she promptly sat down again on the floor and Lola joined her.

And Lola laughing plucked up her mother's book once more and read out the very end of the volume which was most amusing and had perhaps Enid would agree nothing whatsoever to say about faces but was all about sitting on the floor.

Many people are possessed of a great fondness for sitting on the floor, and those who do so will generally give some clue to their character in the way in which they make themselves comfortable in this position.

For instance, should the 'floor-sitter' hug her knees (for these people are generally of the feminine sex) and rock to and fro, she is inclined to be imaginative and given to indulge in flights of fancy. She will more often than not prefer her own society to that of others, and will never be at a loss for amusement when alone.

Should she sit with her legs tucked away under her, she will be youthful and unspoiled in mind; and, indeed, will often prove to be one of those most delightful of people, a 'grown-up child'.

The energetic, clever and impetuous individual will throw herself down on the floor in any attitude, and will fidget and wriggle all the time she is sitting. She is very keen, though apt to be something of a disturbing element at times, owing to her restless, untiring nature.

And, now, if you will follow my rules and facts, you will never be far wrong in your estimation of your fellow-creatures; and it is indeed a comforting notion that we are able to judge others fairly and that we have a safe and reliable guide to the characters and attributes of the people we encounter in our every-day affairs.

It was so funny

It was so extremely funny that the breath of these young floor-sitters almost sisters sifters cysted stopped as clouds curling floated away and this room in the Queen of the Suburbs filled with sun true to no form before witnessed in the miracle of the blossoms of the cherry and almond trees and the great oaks and horse-chestnuts beyond the windows and the sweet swart goblins and gossamer fairies of an undermind in the coronal songs of so many birds both laughing knowing what was about to happen and the sun itself as they sat in its jets and spicules in its surges and flares rim after rim and limb after limb was actually exploding.

LAPIN À LA MOUTARDE

THIS EARLY IN the day, September feels like spring – with the blue still waking in the sky, and the air hazy with bristle fibres from the plane trees. It could almost be pollen or confetti. The sideboard looks ready for something wonderful to happen, with the olive oil standing to attention and those festive sprigs of parsley. Chirac is droning softly through the radio speakers, gracing the kitchen with a presidential address. Then – and isn't this just perfect? – his voice makes way for the march from *Marriage of Figaro*. All tippy toes and dancing skips. I wipe my hands on my apron, fling open the kitchen window wide to share the music with the birds.

Now back to the rabbit's fridge-chilled flesh. So cool against the skin. So soothing for hands still sore from bathroom cleaning – a perfect balm for my bleach burns.

Preparing a welcome meal is not without its pleasures. And a welcome meal for *three*! When Pascal said he was bringing his new girlfriend for lunch, it took all my self-discipline not to set the table there and then. I almost blurted, 'High time!' After all, it's too late to make poor Gérard proud and I'm getting no younger, not to mention Pascal himself. But I kept it all between me and the kitchen walls. 'Give him space,' I told myself, since Gérard is no longer here to remind me, bless his soul.

'Leftovers will do nicely,' is what Gérard would have said to all this fuss.

True, the freezer is still full from Pascal's last aborted visit. But I want this lunch to be just perfect. That's what I'd say, if Gérard were here to listen.

I've a good feeling about Pascal's new girl – something tells me she's a keeper. And there's poetry to Pascal having kept quiet about her these past few months. After all, he was *my* secret for the first twelve weeks of his life. My little treasure, buried safe. Not shared even with Gérard, because I knew by then that to tell Gérard was to tell Belle-mère.

I take a cleaver to the joints.

The rabbit bones crack like my knees.

My fingers gouge mustard from the pot and I daub the pink flesh yellow.

With these knuckles beginning to swell, these purple veins worming beneath the skin, I hardly recognise my hands any more. I could almost believe I was watching Maman working, working . . .

Where did they go, my lovely smooth-skinned hands?

And the rest?

For the table, I'll seat Pascal on my left and his girl on my right – pride of place. I'll dress the table with my wedding linens, white on white. Silver plate, not steel. Crystal, not glass. I'll do better than Belle-mère did by me – I'll treat this girl no less than if she were my own new-found daughter.

If she's the right sort.

I might teach her to make *lapin à la moutarde*, just like Maman taught me.

Well, not *exactly* like Maman taught. There'll be no hauling the rabbit from its pen to hang it head down. No bar to the back of the neck and a bucket of blood. No skinning - one swift tug, like shaking out a sheet. Certainly no sun-drying pelt.

Belle-mère wasted no time teaching me better.

There I was for 'tea', done up in my new collar - as much like marriage material as Maman could make me, by stitching in the mean hours after the day's cleaning jobs. Belle-mère - would-be mother-in-law, then - gave me one look and said, 'Is that *rabbit* fur?' I looked down to hide my blushes. She said no more, as if the shame were so great that was the kindest thing she could do for me.

Scalding it was.

I felt for all the world like these fat rabbit thighs, frying in oil so hot it spits.

After the wedding, Gérard gave me a magnificent beaver stole, all the way from Québec.

'Stunning!' he said, when I tried it on. If I'd managed to catch his eye with a wardrobe of two handmade dresses, I suppose I must have looked quite something in beaver. But I never could wear it.

'I keep thinking of the cost,' I told him.

'You needn't worry,' he said. 'It's Maman's treat.'

To be fair, Gérard made sure I never did have to worry - not about money, at least - but he managed to put his silly, well-meaning finger on the very thing that *was* troubling me. My thoughts had turned to Switzerland - to how costly a gift can be, for the receiver.

I said nothing, though.

We never did speak of Switzerland.

⚜

I'll chop the carrots good and fine.

It's a pleasure to be preparing them as seasoning, rather than main; these veg are all the last girl could have eaten. I'm glad things didn't work out for her and Pascal – between me and the kitchen walls, I can say so. She wasn't the sort for *lapin à la moutarde*. Always pursing her lips in silent judgement, pale eyes peering up from her computer-thing. She was too good for much, with all that learning. Hands so fine it was hard to imagine her wiping her bum, let alone making a bed. Much like Belle-mère. And all for giving me lessons. That time I offered her a blouse, she laid one finger on the fabric and pulled back as if burned. Thinking of Belle-mère offloading cast-offs, I said, 'It's new – just not my size.'

'I wear only natural fibres against my skin,' she said. There I was again. Cheeks blotched with shame. A rabbit-fur collar. Rabbit thighs in hot oil.

This new girl, whatever she's like, is another chance.

If she could be like the very first girl Pascal brought home, wouldn't that be wonderful? He had simpler tastes then – such a sweet, homely girl. Her name's lost to me, but I have a photo – stashed at the back and bottom of my purse. Behind receipts, bank cards. There! Still crumpled from when I saved her from Pascal's waste-paper basket. Dark eyes, sun-browned skin, a gentle smile. It seemed terribly wrong to throw her away.

If I'd had a girl, she might have looked like that.

Chantal, I'd have called her . . .

I'll prop her on the side while I work, like company, and have her gone before Pascal gets here.

There's the rabbit nicely browned.

I bundle it cleanly away beneath an upturned plate, ready for the next step, feeling none of the usual satisfaction – only a sharp little pang. I've begun to feel the burden of things put away, recently. It's as if the attic had started to groan under its load. Even small things weigh heavy. Like how to skin a rabbit – knowledge passed from Mamie, to Maman, to me, then mentioned no more after marriage. That knowledge will be lost, unless I pass it on in turn.

If Pascal's girl is the sort, I'll tell her how Maman gave the rabbit's innards to the dog, but saved the liver – you get a nice big liver on a rabbit. I'll tell her rabbit fur is quite decent, if you harvest it right – soft and warm.

Just the thing for baby boots . . .

Time to put the white wine on to simmer. The glug of it being poured into the pan always feels like a celebration.

But as the heat rises through, the smell rather catches the throat. There's something sinister about those golden heat-glimmers snaking their way up through the liquid. Strings of tiny bubbles streaming to the surface, rushing to escape. In my mind the pan melts, remoulds as glass. The wine becomes warm champagne, and once again I'm on my way to Switzerland.

I can almost hear Gérard's sister Suzette laughing with glee.

Little wonder. What a jaunt! We had bubbles and first-class tickets, thanks to Belle-mère.

'Think of it as a holiday,' Belle-mère had said, and I was

determined to do so - or not to think at all, since thinking could do little good by that point. It was strange, at first, to be travelling with Suzette. She was more envoy than companion, I suppose - guard-cum-guide. We barely knew each other when we set off, but champagne broke the ice, and we were soon thick as thieves. Two runaways.

As we left Avignon, Provence chugged past, with its white crags and poplars jutting into the sky, and the olive trees cowering beneath the mistral. We couldn't leave fast enough for our liking, so we closed the curtains and then it was just us, blood-orange light filtering through the scrim, and dust motes dancing to the rhythm of the train. I felt lightheaded before I'd had even a drop to drink. Everything seemed possible. With one tug we'd blocked out the bold blue skies, the sledgehammer sun, and the stone-melting mistral. For the first time, I was leaving the place I'd been born and raised. Leaving home. No more scraping the bottom of every jar, no more putting aside peelings for soup, no more cutting up every small thing into smaller and smaller pieces so it would go round. I was done coming second to my brother, done handing over wages to poor Maman.

L'échappée belle!

'When you come back, everything will be different,' said Suzette, producing Gauloises to go with the bubbles. 'You and Gérard can do things properly, with a ring, a fairy-tale dress on the big day . . . You could have a billowing skirt and a cinch-waist like Grace Kelly. You'll be perfect, all in white.'

We drank and smoked as if it were already time to celebrate.

The bubbles in our cups kept rising, rising, each one like a promise of more.

Suzette showed me illustrations in a guidebook: mounts

and meadows, the steep rise and fall of the land softened by a fuzz of grasses and wildflowers. Belle-mère had packed guide-books in case of trouble at the border, but looking at those pictures, I was every bit the tourist. It wasn't just Switzerland I was setting out to discover, either – it was a whole new life.

I add the chopped carrots to the wine, plop in a plump garlic bulb, and watch them swirl and churn.

I'm not sure I moved with much more volition back then.

I was terribly young, really.

If life had been less harsh to start with, things might have been different. Belle-mère's talk about pain today for the sake of tomorrow made sense – little different from when we fled the bombings so fast we had to leave the dog. Or when I'd pick out a favourite kitten, knowing that before I got home from school Maman would have turned the rest into limp little bodies, like odd socks still wet from the wash. These days, I often spare a thought for the poor mother cat, prowling and yowling for her lost young, tail whipping the air in fury . . .

I take a blade to the parsley, and feel better for lopping off its hairy green head.

What is certain is that if Belle-mère hadn't been such a *salope* – I can say that too, to the kitchen walls – and with Gérard gone, God rest him – yes, if she hadn't been such a *véritable salope*, Switzerland would never have happened.

When Belle-mère summoned me for 'tea', I was all best behaviour, hoping only for wedding bells. Coming in from the street through those ancient carriage doors, I felt so small. So vulnerable, walking the length of that endless garden path, with its yews and palms lined up like a regiment. I hardly dared press down my heels for fear of messing the raked gravel. At the door, I gave the bell the slightest tug, but still it seemed to echo forever round the many rooms inside before at last opening.

There was Gérard, smiling.

The sight of him was never such a pleasure as then – not even on our wedding day. He was tall, sure. So cultivated in his suit and tie. He took my hand as if I were already his lady-wife and led me inside. Once in the soothing coolness of their entrance hall, standing before the great sweep of staircase, which coiled up three floors at least, I dared believe for the first time in weeks that everything would be fine.

Then Gérard took me in to Belle-mère.

That thought gets my mezzaluna going; I'll make short work of this parsley.

'Poor child!' she said. 'Having to ring like a tradesman! I *specifically* asked for someone to accompany you.' Her apologies left me feeling at fault for an unspecified *faux pas*. I looked to Gérard for guidance, but he had gone; in his place was a boy in Sunday best, looking at his mother as if to ask, 'Is my tie straight? Would you straighten it?'

Belle-mère gave a nod to Gérard, and to me said, 'Please, dear, do sit.'

Gérard led me to a high-backed armchair that left me hemmed in on all sides. He muttered something about us ladies getting better acquainted; his voice strained as if he'd erred into a women's powder room.

And he left.

I must watch myself with the mezzaluna. The blade's a blur.

What *was* he thinking? That mother knew best? That it was *une affaire de femmes*?

Now he's gone, I'll never know.

But I do know this: even when he left me for the great ever-after, I never felt so abandoned as I did that day.

Et voilà: parsley chopped fine as angel's breath.

Belle-mère offered me tea and Harlequin-coloured financiers. She made small talk that somehow sounded grand – great decorous airy sentences that lifted and fluttered like the gauzy curtains at the windows to their garden. It was all so lovely – too lovely. Every 'please' and 'thank you', every delicious bite, every sip from the dainty gold-trimmed cup in my hand left me feeling exposed, as if I was chalking up some mysterious bill; some immense, unpayable debt.

'Gérard explained to me your "delicate situation",' she said eventually.

I looked into my cup, examined the pale brown liquid, the white glow of porcelain beneath.

'More tea?' she said.

I make a start on the shallots, slicing precise, premeditated cuts, still wholeheartedly hating her for that delay.

'*Merci*,' was all I could say. I wanted Maman and her rough ways. It had never occurred to me before then that it was pure kindness, the way she put the rabbits out of their misery so swiftly.

'Gérard intends to do the honourable thing,' said Belle-mère. 'I can count on you to do likewise?'

I thought she meant marriage. Like a fool, I gave a determined nod.

Belle-mère brightened. She spoke about how lucky I was ('A family like ours . . . a girl like you . . .'). How she herself had come up in the world by marrying well. How Gérard would provide properly for his family, now that he had been offered such a promising position as director of the family allocations office.

'I'll make a director's wife of you yet,' she said.

My collar tightened.

Still, it was only when she said, 'Gérard's credibility in his new position would be entirely undermined by any unseemly rush up the aisle,' that the blood drained from my head.

She spoke of 'solutions'. My mind swirled with all the whispered horror stories I'd ever heard: kitchen-table angel makers, knitting needles, rusted iron wires . . . The room tilted. I put down my cup for fear of spilling it.

My eyes smart now as they did that day. If anyone were here to see, I'd blame the shallots.

Belle-mère noticed, back then.

Perhaps she feared I'd refuse to cooperate? She was certainly quick to clarify: 'I would feel uncomfortable sending you anywhere other than Switzerland.' She spoke of specialised clinics where the paperwork could be sorted in advance, told me I needn't worry about the cost - she'd consider it part of the wedding expenses. 'You would be accompanied, of course,' she said. 'Suzette will be there for you.'

The tears came properly then. Perhaps partly from relief that I would be spared a visit to some backstreet kitchen-butchery. Belle-mère's own eyes were red-rimmed, as if the 'solution' was something we had worked out together. Still, when she handed me her handkerchief, I hesitated; it was such a perfect square of pure white cotton, hemmed by tiny stitches and decorated with a fine Calais-lace panel - too beautiful to soil. But when I looked again at those edges, rolled tight and neat as a new leaf, I reached out and took it.

'There, there,' said Belle-mère. Though I hated her for

speaking more softly than Maman ever did, my heart was heavy with thankfulness.

I kept that handkerchief; it seemed understood that I would. It is folded away and so carefully laundered, it looks unused, pristine.

I fry the shallots gently, to keep them sweet.

Add bay leaf to the white wine.

More thyme too, I think.

Think . . .

I didn't, at the time. At least, I tried my hardest not to.

It seems almost grotesque now: Suzette and I giggled and chatted nearly all the way to Switzerland. I suppose we were getting through as best we could.

As we neared the border, Suzette uncovered the windows. 'For the view,' she said. I feared that she was scene-setting – making clear that we had nothing to hide. With the sudden sun in my face, I felt like I'd been pushed onstage, into the spotlight. Or worse, like I'd been shoved into place for an interrogation.

Suzette squeezed my hand.

'We'll have no awkward questions,' she said. 'I know from last time.'

It took me a moment to find the full meaning of her words.

She gazed out the window, raised a hand to her necklace, lifted the pearls from her collar bone. I remembered her boss's generosity paying for her previous Swiss 'holiday'. And the necklace – a gift once she was back behind her typewriter. I understood why she'd been elected as my companion. It came not so much in a flash as on a wave of nausea.

A weighty silence settled between us.

My mind swarmed, suppressed worries rising like the streaming armies of ants in Maman's kitchen. I was on the brink of choking out, 'I'm not sure about this.' But Suzette spoke first, filling the awkward silence as people so often do, with that little joke about an angel passing: '*Un ange passe!*'

She refilled my cup though it wasn't empty, and proposed a toast: 'Here's to better to come!'

When we arrived, it did seem that there might be better days ahead. Everything at the clinic was so new and white, so bright and clean. Like a smart hotel – at least, like the smart hotels I had imagined. There were nurses everywhere asking, 'Is Madame comfortable? Shall I get you anything?' It seemed too late to reply other than with a smile and a shake of the head.

I add the rabbit to the shallots, pour in the white wine mixture.
Almost done.

Into the oven it goes, to cook properly: long and slow. *Securely lidded.*

I felt much the same when I woke at the clinic: hospital corners held the sheets in place so firmly, I was all but bound to the bed. And still those gentle voices asked, 'Is Madame comfortable? Can I get anything for Madame?' If I could have, I'd have asked for everything to be undone. But I fell asleep again, and dreamt of wedding robes, and funeral shrouds, and my future mother-in-law tucking me in too tight.

⁂

- Hello, my *chou*. What time will you be in?
    - Ah? Not the high-speed train? If you check, you might

155

still be able to get a quicker train from Nîmes. I made your favourite.

- *Lapin à la moutarde*, of course! It should be ready by one-thirty.

- I see. Well, you and I could eat the rabbit, and I could prepare a salad for . . . Katy. Katy? She's not French then?

- That's a bit much, darling. I'm sure she'll understand that, here, rabbit is no different from any other meat. She might be curious to discover regional cooking.

- Well, yes. In that case, I can see it might seem *like* offering stewed dog or cat. Still, a farmed rabbit is not the same as a pet.

- No, no, I *do* see. I'll put it away for another day. Another time.

- When will you be in?

- There's plenty to see and do right here. Katy might like to see Avignon Bridge, the Pope's palace . . .

- No that's fine. Nîmes is lovely, it's true.

- No, it's fine. Next week is fine. Really.

※

With the sky clouded over, the fibres from the plane trees look less like confetti – more like the dried flowers the undertakers gave out at Gérard's funeral to scatter on his grave. And with the warmth gone out of the day, that's a cruel mistral.

As I shut the window, the wind blasts in for a last swagger round the kitchen, rifling papers, picking up and dropping the photo of that dear girl. There's no panic to tidy her away, now that Pascal's not coming. I reach out to prop the picture up again, but my hand falters. I settle for letting the picture lie flat on the sideboard, thinking to get on with the next steps of the recipe – the cream, the lemon juice . . . But it seems so stupid, futile, to fill an already full freezer.

Another option: I could do away with the whole damn lot.

Let the wind take the photo.

Throw away the meal.

But I feel that curious lightness I first felt in Switzerland, like I've been cored – a small, deep emptiness. I'm bored right through with it. I lower myself into a chair, its legs and mine creaking in protest. I take a breath in, a breath out. And I sit. Listening to the rabbit simmering, for a child that won't come.

MINOR DISTURBANCES

'STAND BACK, MIKEY.'

Penny knew better than to pull her child away. His hands were on the window that looked out from the Fun Court - the glass ran from floor to ceiling. He leaned in, waved at a distant tractor outside; the field it ploughed extended from the fence beneath the window to the horizon. This leisure mall, with its play centre, its pool and gym, was on the city's outskirts, hard up against farmland. The tractor towed some sort of plough; a gauze of dust surrounded it. Some rain had fallen but still, everything looked very dry.

The child banged his fist on the glass.

'Nearly time to go in,' Penny coaxed. Distraction was the best way to manage him.

He kept his hand on the glass, but he turned to face the play centre. It contained three levels all connected by slides, the whole thing contained within a swathe of nylon mesh. Inside, the edges of everything were softened so the children would not hurt themselves - vinyl-covered sponge, wipe-clean cushions, foam-wrapped bars. The man who supervised the entrance was young and very overweight, skin pallid, hair thin in a way that suggested deficiency despite his excess flesh. Penny knew his name - 'Jonah'.

Every week Penny met friends from her post-natal group here. They'd been coming for several years – now their children were nearly four. They'd drive out, winding their windows in accordance with the official advice, filters on their highest setting. Unlike the play centres in town, there were no rules here about bringing your own food. You could eat at the tables dotted around the café. You didn't even need to buy a coffee, but Penny always did. It was her weekly luxury.

Today it was just her and Caroline.

On a napkin she arranged a neat pile of carrot sticks, a handful of garden peas.

'What have you brought for Leonore?' she asked Caroline.

'Just bread sticks today,' Caroline said.

Penny wanted to roll her eyes. She wished Jen was here, or Sharon, with whom she could share a secret smile. Caroline's daughter rarely joined the children in the play centre, instead sitting in a beanbag in the 'quiet zone', turning the pages of a picture book. The child had an austere manner, which Caroline indulged. *She's very self-contained*, she'd crow.

Penny beckoned to Mikey. 'Nearly time.' When he came to her, she gave him a carrot stick.

'Eat this and then you can go in,' she said.

But Mikey tucked the carrot into his palm, sloped towards Jonah.

From her bag, Penny retrieved a small pot of dip. She popped the lid, held it out.

'Mikey,' she called, 'you can dip your carrot in this.'

'What's that?' Caroline leaned across the table.

'Hummus, from that supermarket on Causewayside. They didn't have many.' Penny kept a tight hold of the tub. 'They were putting them out as I arrived. Lucky timing.'

'Is it good?' Caroline asked.

'It ought to be for what they charged.' Penny sighed. 'It's for Mikey, really. I worry about what he's missing out on.'

Like most children, Mikey was nourished in line with the official advice, which was to encourage normal eating, for the situation was not permanent. This 'situation' was that food like the carrots and peas Penny had brought today contained only trace nutrients. The real problem was that they tasted of nothing. Penny added the vital supplements to prevent malnutrition, laying Mikey's meals out on starchy fortified bread, adding the recommended powders to pasta, to potatoes. But how to encourage a child to *eat normally*?

Penny knew Caroline wanted to taste the hummus, but she didn't offer. *It's for Mikey*, she repeated to herself, though she'd already sampled some, seeking garlic, lemon, finding only a poor imitation.

'C'mon, Mikey,' she cajoled.

But Mikey placed his carrot on the floor, then dashed past Jonah and into the play centre.

Today, Caroline fetched the coffee; Penny remained seated, watching Mikey.

'They make the foam so creamy,' Caroline said, depositing the tray.

Penny took her cup, sipped at the coffee. The colour was perfect, but the drink was thick and bland, tasting neither of coffee nor milk.

Through the window, the tractor that Mikey had watched earlier appeared larger, having reached the middle of the field. Behind it, the wind sucked up thin topsoil, sudden gusts producing turbid clouds. Perhaps there would be a storm. Penny imagined traces of dust in her car, the scent seeped through the filters, a desperate phosphate hum. She searched the field for pigeons or crows, even gulls – the minor disturbances they might create picking about for worms or seeds. But perhaps they didn't like the murky air.

'Can I try some of your dip?' Caroline's bald request took Penny by surprise. She held tightly to the pot while Caroline dipped a breadstick, assessed the taste as if recalling a ritual. 'It's quite zingy,' she observed, 'but I doubt that's lemon.' There were still cooking programmes, exhorting viewers to try this, add that, advising substitutes for ingredients no longer available. It had been strange watching them while pregnant, when everything Penny ate had a strange mineral tang. TV chefs smacking their lips, observing texture, temperature, colour. Only after Mikey was born did Penny notice how rarely they observed taste. For much of what came out of the earth now tasted of almost nothing. Even meat, when available, evoked little more than the waxy notes of what the beast had been fed.

Caroline coated another breadstick, then Penny replaced the lid. She searched vaguely for Mikey inside the play centre, remembering how once a little boy had scaled the outside of the soft-strong fence. He'd lain face down in the broad hammock of its roof, arms out across the netting, like he was flying. Security staff had to come and retrieve him. Penny couldn't see Mikey now, but she wasn't too concerned.

She popped a pea into her mouth, listening for the taste, moving it around and thinking of the zones of the tongue – sweet, sour, bitter, salt. Mostly the pea was powdery marrow. Potatoes were gluey, tomatoes, at their best, benignly acidic. Penny seasoned before serving, as advised – there was no shortage of salt – only it made you so thirsty and the water tasted strange, even after boiling and filtering. That was the advice – it wouldn't make you ill, but to make it more drinkable, boil and if necessary, strain.

Leonore rose from the beanbag now and approached the table.

Penny craned her neck. 'Did Mikey come past you?'

'Oh, yes,' Leonore said, matter-of-factly. 'But I don't know where he went.' She lifted a breadstick delicately to her mouth.

'Check with Jonah,' Caroline advised.

Penny rose, strode towards the mesh. 'Mikey?' she called, walking along beside it, peering in at the climbing frame, the slides. Her coffee was at the top of her gullet – 'Mikey?'

Jonah eased his body from behind the desk, ambled over and stood, rocking on his heels.

'I can go in and look?' he offered.

Penny let her eyes move over his frame. 'I'd rather do it myself,' she said.

She swished past him.

'You haven't removed your shoes,' Jonah called after her.

Mikey was not on the swings or in the sport zone. He was not hanging off the bars or lying in the tunnel. Penny even searched the netted ceiling.

'I'll check the toilets,' she called to Caroline.

On her way, she passed the viewing platform overlooking the pool. The swimmers cut their way through the treated water. Their caps shone; their arms glistened. She turned away – Mikey would never be able to negotiate his way near the pool.

At the women's toilets, Penny flung open the door, calling out. Inside, only one cubicle was occupied, not the one Mikey

liked to use when she brought him in with her. He was a creature of habit, suspicious about any kind of change in routine,
especially when emptying his bladder. She tapped on the
door.

'He's not in here,' came a voice.

Tears were at the back of Penny's throat, instead of behind
her eyes. She wondered vaguely what they'd taste of if she
wept.

The walk back felt endless, legs loose, heart squeezed. Penny
did not see Caroline at the coffee booth until Caroline called
out to her. She was holding Leonore's hand.

'Penny, Leonore just told me she saw Mikey at the window
when we were drinking our coffee. If he came around the far
side it'd be easy to miss him.'

Beside Caroline, the child stood, calm, smiling, as if pleased
with herself, Penny thought. She pictured those breadsticks.
Caroline never let anyone see Leonore refuse food. It was
almost certainly why she didn't bring carrots or cucumber,
peppers or peas. Apparently, Leonore ate hers at home. Penny
bit her tongue. How she hated them both right now, the im-
permeable unit they presented holding tight to each other, as
if the world they'd all arrived in could not touch them.

'Penny,' Caroline said, very gently. 'It's possible Mikey went
back in to play. You should check.'

Penny returned to the play centre, but she didn't go inside this
time. Instead, she tried to sense rather than search for Mikey.
Her thoughts flashed and strobed. She remembered a child
safety video her mother-in-law once showed her. You must
be alert to silence, as much as sound, it advised, to stillness

as well as movement. A drowning child, for instance – it will not splash or call out but will slip quietly beneath the surface of the water. Penny turned again in the direction of the pool, but as she passed the window, the tractor – now so close that the view was blurred by dust – slowed and stopped, and Penny slowed and stopped too. Inside the cab, the driver, visible at this distance, stared, gaze angled down. At a child?

'He's out there,' Penny said, hardly believing it.

But how? Staring around her now, she noted the vast windows, allowing so much light – but they didn't open. And there was no exterior door on this level – Penny turned, searched wildly – not a single door. How had he got out? How would she get him back?

She turned towards the distant exit doors. The carpark. Of course. It was underground, where they entered and exited every week. Mikey knew the way.

She turned, prepared to dash across the forecourt, only now, Caroline was standing right beside her, very close, and Penny noticed she was with someone, a woman, robed, wearing a swim-cap.

'I saw your boy,' the woman said. 'Heading into the toilets.'

'I already checked there.' Penny's voice was small and distant. 'He's outside.' She put her fingers in her mouth, as if by doing so she might contain her distress, she might cram it back into her body. Here came the tears.

'No. I saw him,' the woman insisted. She was pointing.

There it was, the thing Penny had not seen, for the woman was not indicating the door Penny expected.

Something shifted, settled into place. She moved quickly now in the right direction.

In the men's toilet, with its limey tang, was Mikey, pants

half-hitched, before a sink full of soapy water. 'I'm nearly finished,' he informed her.

'Come here, love,' she said. 'I'll help you.'

Mikey returns to the play centre, Penny to her tepid coffee. When Leonore reaches for the tub of hummus, Penny opens the lid. Offers it to Caroline too. Then she eats one of Mikey's carrots, and imagines the journey home, windows wound, filters on their highest setting, how Mikey will sleep, and she'll check the fields as she drives. She promises herself she'll pull over if she sees anything at all - a flicker in the dirt - a crow, a pigeon, a gull. She'll watch carefully, recalling how when she wept, the taste of her tears was familiar, uncomplicated, the weight of them there again now, as if they'd never left her body.

TIMOTHY J JARVIS

TO HAVE A HORSE

YOU WORK ON it during the hours of darkness, on some waste ground abandoned to witchgrass, cow parsley, yarrow, nettle, and scrub alder and willow, at the edge of town, past a railway siding and brakes of briar. Once, long ago, there was a workshop on the site that made soft-whip ice cream machines, and you sometimes stumble over half a decaying brick or turn up, with the toe of your boot, a nozzle that glints in the starlight.

The moon goes from full, through new, and back to waxing gibbous before you're finished. Some nights it's above you, looking down on your work, on others it never rises, or is hidden behind a high thick wrack of cloud scudding away to the west. Each dusk you walk out of town, cross the tracks of the siding, threading the abandoned commuter trains, canted carriages splashed with tags, once garish, now dull, faded, and pick your way through the tangle of mallow and bramble. And each dawn you return. Sometimes under a sky the colour of salmon left too long on the fishmonger's slab, sometimes under a sulphuric haze.

And then one night, clear, with a spatter of stars and that mangled moon overhead, you realise it's ready. An armature as if of bone cobbled from twisted spars of dull metal scavenged from the wreckage of the old car plant. Joints moulded from a putty made from boiling up squirrel and rat carcasses, then scraping the residue out of the pot. Sinews of rusting barbed wire. All draped with a mould-furred tarpaulin. The skull is two pieces of hard grey plastic from the casing of an old photocopier carved in clumsy apery of the wicked bone callipers of a real horse's skull, jaw articulated with baling twine. It stands tottering on swollen hocks, as if afflicted with bog spavin. Had it been real, a horse like this would have been sent to the shambles or the glue factory. But there are no real horses, which is why you have made this sham.

You clear a patch of earth and start a small fire with the smashed pieces of an old table you've been saving. For kindling, you light a hank of steel wool cupped in your hands, before tucking it into the nest of broken-up timber. It burns quickly and like a tracery of burst blood vessels, then flinders away to nothing. But you blow softly and steadily, and sparks puff up, and before long the wood catches. Then you stop and intone the invocation you found in the old book (and which you spent some days translating from medieval Latin with the aid of a primer taken from a classroom of the public school in town):

I conjure you demons from the south,
And by the seven frogs and these winds;
I conjure and adjure you:
That you should speedily and without delay,
And without deception,
Terror and trembling and injury to my body,
Bring me a horse prepared and ready to do my will.

Then you sit down by the fire and wait. Staring into the flames, you think about how you used to now and again feel, as a jolt, the interconnectedness of things. Of the squabbling starlings, chittering blackbirds, and tits that perched in the bushes of your back garden; of the mangy one-eyed fox that often skulked at the foot of it and survived on kebab leftovers and fried chicken bones; of the scurrying rats in the alley-way that ran down one side of your house; of the tangle of dogrose, hawthorn, and poppy of your frail elderly neighbour's overgrown garden, and of the midges, mosquitoes, blowflies, wasps, and bees that whined, droned, and buzzed through this thicket, alighting on red and pinkish blossoms, russet berries; of the dead hare in a nest of thorns and the pallid grubs that made the carcass to shimmer; of the kite that soared, circling, overhead, its shrill piping like the whistle of an old-fashioned kettle; of the newts and frogs in the storm sewer off down towards the river; of the bream, roach, perch, and tench swim-ming in its waters; of the flukes burrowing into their flesh; of the knot of elver squirming in the shadow of the bank a little way upstream; of all the people going about their days or nights, sleeping, eating, working, drinking, arguing, fucking, and lying benumbed or rapt before the coruscations of the TV; and of the inanimate too, the housing estates, all the derelict industrial buildings, the air, the sun and moon, the blue sky and the clouds, and the scattering of stars that could faintly be seen, points of light in a net of contrails, in the west of the lightening sky.

But now everything is a smash-up, a wreck, and there are just strewn shards and splinters.

After some time you start, thinking you see a glimmer in

the socket of the skull you roughly hewed, but it is only fire-light glistering from the threads of a web a spider has swiftly spun there. In the end, bone-weary and lulled by the wavering flames, their faint warmth in the night's chill, you can't keep awake, your chin falls to your chest, and you slump forward.

You wake up screaming. Somehow the fire has spread to your hair and jacket. Running stumbling about the waste ground, you bat at your head and chest with your hands, before throwing yourself down in a sump at its edge to hiss and steam. When you get to your feet again, your hair is mostly gone, your hands and scalp are blistered, and the manmade fibres of your jacket have melted into a thick carapace. Then you remember the dream you were woken from.

In it you were somewhere else, at another time, at some kind of festival in a country village. The Carousing of the Grey Mare. A rabble went through the streets from house to house, following a man leading, by reins of woven bramble, a figure draped in a sheet, blue with gold stars, who held aloft on a pole the yellowed skull of a horse, adorned with ribbons and tatters that streamed behind in the wind. In the sockets of the skull had been placed two white flowers like trumpets, which gave off a cloying scent of nectar and dung.

At each house the leader would knock on the door while the Mare pranced up and down, its lower jaw clacking, and the mob would chant, with one voice and the solemnity of a liturgy, an old folk song of some sort:

Bonefaced, with eyes of stars,
Deathless and dark-matter shod,

Gravid have I been
Since spores first drifted cross the void
And seeded this spinning ball of clay.
But now I feel the birthing pangs,
And seek a place to foal.
Won't you let me in?

You sit on the cold ground, in your shell of char, the stink of burnt hair, skin, and plastic in your nostrils, looking out into the girding dark and musing on the meaning of this dream.

Some time will pass, then you'll see a brief slash of light over-head. And at the same moment, hear a faint whickering from behind you. Your breath will catch in your throat and your eyes will fill with tears. Without looking round, you'll incant the second part of the formula from the old book:

O good horse I conjure you
By Dedya, Stelpha, Draco, Drogancio, Barabas,
And Medya, who is the mistress,
And he who rides upon a black mount,
And she, upon a red,
That you may have neither in your body,
Nor in your mind,
Nor in the most unclean part of your body
The will to make me fall at all,
But that you should bear me to my place
Healthy and uninjured,
According to my will.

Then you'll wait a moment before turning, all the while

thinking about the journey ahead, the hard time you'll have of it, that which awaits you at its end, and about the last time you cried, so long ago, on that night when you choked on the salt tang of blood or brine and the cloying perfume of bindweed flowers.

CLAIRE CARROLL

THE SUN IS ONLY A SHIPWRECK INSOFAR AS A WOMAN'S BODY RESEMBLES IT

ANDRÉ BRETON IS staying over at the beach house. It's unbearably hot. I wake from a nap, with the heat pressing in, and he's standing over me with a box of hair dye he has found in the bathroom cabinet.

Let's do this, he says.

The sheets are damp. I fell asleep in my swimsuit. I sit up and take the box. The label says: 'Lightest Ash Blonde'. The cardboard is soft at the corners. The image of a smiling woman on the front is cracked and faded; she looks ethereal, delirious, old.

This looks old, I tell him, but he gestures at me to be quiet.

He sits down in the chair that faces the dressing table, draping a towel around his shoulders. There's a little container in the box, into which I must pour the liquid part of the dye and a sachet of powder. I mix the two substances together with a plastic wand. André Breton smokes impatiently and

172

looks out of the window. The tide is out; the sand stretches away and away, succumbing to uneven towers of black and pink sparkling rock that poke at the sky. There are white clouds gathering on the horizon. We'll have a walk soon, when we've done this; when it's cooler outside. The liquid and powder form a paste. The texture is gritty. A violent ammonia smell rises from the plastic container. The curtains at the window hang motionless in the thick, hot air. It's unbearably hot.

André Breton is looking at himself in the mirror, he's wearing a white cotton vest because of the heat. It's unbearably hot. He has taken off his glasses and placed them neatly on the table. He has this tension in his back and neck and shoulders; his muscles appear to be permanently flexed, like he can't relax. He's been like this since he arrived. He won't let me help him though; he won't let me touch him. There is supposed to be some sort of application brush in the box, but it's missing.

There's no application brush in the box, I tell André Breton.

He peers inside to confirm. He rarely takes my word for things. He sighs. I stand behind him and we look at each other in the mirror for a long time. His hair is dark and thick, just like in his pictures. It's not until decades later, when he's much older, that it lightens to grey. I touch the tops of his arms as softly as I can. Testing to see if he flinches. He doesn't. I press more firmly. When I release my fingertips, there are oval marks on his skin. I wait as they dissolve into him. He nods.

You can just use your hands, he says.

There are no gloves in the box. So I scoop up small globs of the white, viscous dye with my bare fingers and start to work them through his hair. I begin with the roots. The dye stings my bitten cuticles, but I don't mind. At first, it's clear that André Breton doesn't like me touching his scalp. His shoulders tauten. From my position close to the back of his head, I can see – feel – the hard right-angle of his clenched jaw. But as I work the dye through his hair – carefully, gently – he begins to relax.

See, this is good, I say as I check to see if the dye covers every strand of his hair, *this feels important*.

He doesn't answer but he gives me a tiny, reluctant smile in the mirror. We have to wait forty-five minutes before washing off the dye. We decide to go and sit outside on the sun loungers. André Breton goes first, and we walk through the hallway to the kitchen-diner. I wash my hands. The water fizzes over the raw skin on my palms. I fill a jug with water and ice and put it on a tray with two glasses. I carry the tray towards the patio doors. They are open, and the drapes on either side hang motionless in the thick, hot air. It's unbearably hot. The grass in the garden is coarse and dry underfoot, like scorched rope. Beyond, the rocks, the sand, the sand, the endless sand and the invisible sea.

The sun loungers wait in the shade of the pine trees that loom over the beach house from the cliffs behind. Nothing much grows here at this time of year, but what does is stiff, succulent. André Breton and I put on our sunglasses and sit down. The slick dye glistens. I can see, already, his dark hair turning blond.

Your hair is turning blond, I say.

He smiles and produces a bottle from his trouser pocket, pours a pale green, cloudy liquid into our two glasses, tops them up with water. We sip our drinks – they taste like cut grass – and the little garden shimmers. André Breton reaches over for my hand, and I stretch towards him. I close my eyes and my arm keeps stretching and my fingers reach into his hair. My nails scrape at his scalp where the glassy dye is congealing in the heat of the day, and I feel like my fingers could go right through the skin, through his skull and into his brain. Then I'd know things about him that no one else knows. I open my eyes. André Breton doesn't seem to mind me touching him now. In fact, he seems to like it. When he opens his mouth, slightly, there's something in there. It looks like another garden. The garden looks like this one, but it's late spring. Everything is new and fresh; the tide is high and blue and cold. I let go of his scalp, take off my sunglasses for a better look. He removes his sunglasses too, looks me in the eye directly for the first time since he arrived at the beach house. He leans forward, takes hold of my hand.

You're covered in dye again, he says.

He pulls me towards him and lifts the hem of his white vest so that he can use it to clean my fingers. I leave my sun lounger for him to do this, and crouch at his feet in the dry, dead grass. From this angle, his face eclipses the sun. I begin to tell him this, but my mouth is too dry. I watch him carefully as he cleans under my nails and in between my fingers, taking care with each one in turn. It's almost too much to bear. But then he stops. There's a ringing noise from inside; the phone, an alarm maybe. It's time to wash off the dye. He leaps up and runs inside.

I peel myself up from the ground and walk to the edge of the garden. There's a little fence at the end, with a gate that swings on its hinges like a loose tooth. It opens straight on to the sea wall. A little way along there are steps down to the sand. The shoreline is empty. No one visits this beach; it's too terrifying. At low tide, the water is so far away that you forget it's there. You can walk for miles between rocks that grow and grow the further you drift from the land. There are rockpools that will swallow you whole. There are dark towers of seaweed, their insides tangled around dead birds, cuttle-fish bones, trawler nets, Lego bricks, lone flipflops, cigarette filters, tossed engagement rings, false teeth, glass eyes. When it turns, the water sneaks vindictively back to the land. If you were to stay out too long, you'd be stranded. But at high tide the water is too close. It laps at the sea wall, slops into the garden, hurries up to the patio doors. In the winter, you dream all night of the beach house rising infinitely on the brimming tide.

André Breton's hands appear from behind and rest at my sides. I lean into him. He is cool from the shower. His hair is still wet; it drips onto my shoulders. I close my eyes and reach around to the back of his neck; the muscles feel so much looser than they did earlier.

AN INVOCATION

CAN I GET a red wine, darling?

Thanks. Okay, shall we start?

Right, good evening. It's an honour to be invited to speak here today. I don't usually find myself in such esteemed surroundings. I'm going to be talking about a photograph I took of the great James Dee in 1973, shortly before his untimely demise. Or rather, I should say, his untimely disappearance. Maybe he's still out there somewhere. Let's hope so.

Here it is, on the screen behind me.

Not bad, is it?

It's my most-reproduced photograph. Someone once said it was on the wall of a million teenage bedrooms, which is a humbling thought. I'm supposed to say something about how I made it and why I think it's a successful photograph and why it has had the impact it has. We'll get on to that. But first I'll give you some context.

The band was at the peak of their powers. They'd just released their third album, *Voodoo Mother, Demon Brother,* and it was clearly something very special. Without compromising their vision in the slightest, they had somehow nailed the crossover. They were on what would have been their last tour of what we might call mid-sized venues, the theatres and the uni halls. After this it was going to be stadiums and arenas. America. The big time. The very big time.

I'd met the band and photographed them a few times before, even right at the beginning, and I'd always found them good company. Down to earth, nice blokes. We'd enjoyed a few drinks together. Dee – Jim – and I got on okay. He was pretty intense company and saw himself as an 'artist', which of course he was. To be honest, I was closer to Nick and the others. The pleasures of the road and all that. You know what I'm saying. Anyway, this time round it was immediately clear something had changed. The atmosphere around them was dense. It was charged. And it wasn't just that everyone, from the management to the promotors to the road crew, knew that they were about to go supernova. No, it was something else. Hard to explain really. There was a heaviness.

I wondered if it was the drugs. Of course, later on there were the rumours of black magic and that absurd court case in the US. And all of that was encouraged by the weird circumstances around Dee's disappearance.

Anyway, by the time I hooked up with the tour he was *crackling*. Really, you had the feeling that if you touched him – and Jesus, a lot of people wanted to touch him – you would get an electric shock.

I was hired by the magazine to shoot three concerts towards the end of the tour: Birmingham, Manchester, and then the finale at the Royal Albert Hall. They were going to do a big special. Cover feature, interview with Jim, review of the tour, and so on. Usually for those jobs I had one night and would roam around and take pictures from different places. Play it by ear, find the good angles. Every venue is different and every performance is new so you have to react. But this time, I thought I would be very disciplined and focus on one position each evening. I had an inkling that they were building to something special for the final night and so I thought I would save the pit photos for then. That's the position you tend to get the best head shots from, the close ups.

The Birmingham gig was good. Really good. I remembered then what a great band they were live. I was at the side of the stage and I took about five rolls while they were on stage. Then another roll backstage in the dressing rooms. I thought I had some good shots but afterwards, when I developed the films, about half of them were blank. And the others were ruined by these weird flares and burns, a bit like you get when film is exposed to radiation. Couldn't explain it. Faulty film, perhaps. Very odd.

The second night I was concentrating on what I call the big picture shots: the whole stage, the band in full flight, the light show. Wide angle. Management got me access to one of the opera boxes up and to the side, and I got some great angles looking down from there, and then went down and was taking views from the side of the stage and through the backline and drum kit: the band, their backs to me, and the sea of faces beyond. The unholy congregation. The sense of devotion, of worship even, was incredible. But then the strap on my camera snapped and the case cracked open on the floor, exposing the film. I started to feel the job was cursed. Of course, I had a couple of cameras, all with different lenses, but that was the one I thought had the best shots. It was a strange accident. Never happened before and never happened since. At the end I had some okay images from that night but nothing of the individual members of the band. So the pressure was on me for the finale at the Royal Albert Hall.

On the day the sense of expectation was massive. When I arrived to check out the venue and the angles – this was hours before they opened the doors – there were huge crowds outside already. Some of the kids had gone over the road into Hyde Park and had lit fires. There were police. You could feel the tension and anticipation. You just knew it was going to be one of those seminal gigs. You know, one of the ones that everyone says they were at.

When they came on it was clear they wanted to make a statement. Given my run of bad luck I was super careful with my kit and hoped I would get some good pictures.

They were brilliant. Committed, tight, electric. The climax of the gig was a massive version of 'Maelstrom'. Everyone knows that track now; the single is one of those classics that you find on pub jukeboxes and even hear on drivetime radio shows. But that version is heavily edited compared to the album track, and live it was a very different beast again.

In the middle section, which even on the album version has just a short guitar solo, they would do something very different. There is a descending sequence of chords, down through the octave alternating majors and minors, hitting the so-called Devil's Interval, the *Diabolus in Musica*, the tritone, the unholy flatted fifth, and then at the bottom of the octave looping round again, so that it feels as if the descent goes on and on, down and down and down. And at that time, when they did it live, they would lock into that loop and just keep going. No solos. Just layers of noise, building. It was incredible. Very very heavy. It just went on and on. And when you thought that surely it had gone on too long and they were about to break back into the chorus, it would go on even more and if anything would have even more intensity and volume. Nick, Johnny, and Mac would be locked into their groove, at the back of the stage by the drum riser, all with their heads down. In the zone. And James Dee would go into full shaman mode, dancing, whirling, exhorting the front rows of the audience and gesturing deep into the darkness of the auditorium, pulling the audience to come unto himself. Great stuff. Magnetic. Powerful.

The audience would go nuts and the lighting guy would throw everything at it, strobes and so on, which made it a nightmare for me. With the lights and the dry ice and every-thing else it was almost impossible to see what I was shooting so I just pointed and clicked and hoped for the best. You may laugh, but it's the truth. We don't always know what we're doing.

There's a lot of luck in photography.

So we were in the maelstrom, descending and descending, on a wild helter-skelter ride, heading into the heart of dark-ness, and Dee was spinning in the centre of the stage like a dervish. Spinning and spinning. And it seemed to me there was a darkness there, a gathering of density around him. And I swear I saw flames. I thought it was part of the show but afterwards the manager, who had seen them too, said it wasn't. But the stage was definitely scorched. There were burn marks, like someone had kindled a campfire right there on the stage. The roadcrew puzzled over that later on when they disman-tled everything.

Well, that's the story. Let's take a look at the image. Of course it has been so popular because of the expression on his face. That's why it's been so successful as a poster. Look at him. Handsome devil.

We can talk about film stock and printing and so on but

I can't really say anything about the technical aspect of the shoot, f-stops and exposures and all that. Shooting in that situation is very intuitive. In the moment, when it's happening, I'm really just improvising. And at that moment, like I said, with the strobes and smoke bombs and everything, I was almost shooting blind. They say you make your own luck, and on that night I was obviously lucky. The framing is perfect, even if I say so myself. I didn't have to crop at all when it came to the printing.

But what I think is so extraordinary is this. Here. Can you see? The second figure? Must be eight feet tall. I'm always surprised by how many people don't see it. Of course, once you've seen it you can't unsee it. But is it just a glitch in the image, shadows and light and reflections, or was he really there? I don't know, I really don't.

But I do know something in the air changed as the music spiralled down into the depths. We all felt it. And honestly, for a moment there, I felt absolutely terrified. I was in the presence of something I couldn't really see but which I could definitely feel. Maybe it was just the music, or maybe not. Whatever it was, it was awesome. I've spoken to a few people who were there, both crew and kids who were in the audience, and we all felt the same thing. It was like something entered the building. For a moment I saw the darkness forming and clinging to Jim, like smoke, wrapping around him like a shroud. And his face, I could see that he was terrified too. You know when you're on a roller coaster and the penny drops that it is going to be way more scary than you thought? It was like that. Of course, in the picture, it looks like he is in ecstasy. Photographs can lie.

And of course, there were other photographers there that

night and other pictures. But this is the only one where you can see that second figure.

It was a hell of a concert. 'Maelstrom' seemed to go on for hours and it was amazing. Like being hit by a truck. The sound was at eleven, for sure. When they brought it to a close it was like the venue had been turned upside down by an earthquake. When the sound stopped there was a moment of silence and it was like a vacuum, like the air had been sucked out of the space.

The audience were broken. But they were still calling for more.

Normally, the band would come back on for an encore (they usually did 'Possession' and a really early song like 'Nerve Endings'), but that night it just wasn't possible. They had given everything. There was a weird stillness. I looked back out into the crowd and saw that half a dozen people had passed out. Others were literally on their knees, weeping. As the smoke began to clear, the lighting guy put up the lights on the crowd and turned off the lights on the stage. It was the end.

Backstage, in the dressing rooms, Dee was already locked away and wouldn't see anyone. He'd come off stage in a real state apparently. The stage manager said he looked haunted. That was his exact word: *haunted*. The others were in a state of shock. Later, Nick told me he'd felt something pass through them. He'd felt that something had been released. And because of that he was working on a bottle of Scotch and a massive reefer. To bring himself down, as he said. Johnny kept on saying he needed oxygen. More air, more air. Mac was out cold on the floor in a corner.

We all know what happened next.

I never saw James Dee again. And incredibly, it seems this is actually the last picture ever taken of him. When, after he had gone, the band decided to do a 'best of' album, they used my image on the cover. And that was that. A million bedrooms.

So, any questions?

ROSIE GARLAND

WHAT BUSINESS HAS A HORSE TO LOOK DOWN ON ME?

THE HORSE IS in the kitchen again. Beats me how when I lock every door and window. I concentrate on washing up, grinding a scouring pad in circles to shift burnt-on rice. The horse shakes its head, flapping the damp velvet of its lips. I refuse to turn, because that would acknowledge its existence. It sneezes snot onto the tiled floor.

Snort all you like, buster, I think, attacking the pan with a knife.

My father said horses were God's most perfect creatures. *Steady and reliable,* he said, wrong in that piece of wisdom as he was in everything. The closest he got to steady was shedding his wages on a slow stumbler who fell at the first fence.

Cats are the best animal. They can squeeze under doors, climb curtains. No one can show me a horse clever enough to do that, not with their constant demands for attention, finicky appetites, rolling eyes. Cats taught me how to need no one, not ever.

The horse taps a hoof, muscles quivering along the russet

sheen of its flanks. If I continue to ignore it, it will leave. I'm good at ignoring, like I ignore the last time I saw my father and the words we screamed at each other, burned hard like rice on a pan.

They say the apple doesn't fall far from the tree. Depends how steep the slope. Soon as I could, I rolled down my hill, further and further away, picking up speed until apple trees and horses were less than specks of dirt in my eye, nothing a bit of salt water couldn't wash away.

I hurl the ruined pan into the filthy dishwater and stride into the hall, button up my coat. The horse trots after, glances at my laced-up boots, shakes its mane coquettishly. If that's what it wants, it can have it. I open the door.

Go on, I snarl. *Do us both a favour and sod off.*

I'd say it's sulking but horses can't smile, or frown, or anything else that counts as an expression. I slam the door so forcefully I loosen the hinges a little more. I shrug off the coat, head to the bathroom and slide the bolt. The horse is ahead of me. It leans against the bath, scenting the room with straw.

I've tried to work out when it first arrived. I'm sure I came home one day and there it was, nose shoved in a box of teabags, but memories slide away when I cling too tightly.

It takes a clopping step, rests the massive block of its head on my shoulder. I won't buckle. Won't let it know I'm weighed down, because then I'd have to stop. I'd have to remember when I had dreams of walking into my first job and flying up the ladder. Friends and parties and open roads stretching to a horizon without hills and nothing to mess up the view.

The horse lets out a sigh, treacly and warm. It shouldn't be me who has to change. I asked for nothing, certainly not a horse following me around, flapping its huge eyelashes and making pitying noises at the back of its throat.

And if, just if, I put in all the hard work and thankless slog at sorting out my life, I'd have to stop slamming doors. I'd have to turn around and look the horse in the eye. I'd have to speak kind words, lay my arm around its neck, let it lead me out the back door and show me how the garden is bursting with new life this time of year and then who would be left to clear up all this shit.

KERRY HADLEY-PRYCE

CUL-DE-SAC

IT'S STILL LIGHT when the taxi pulls up outside the house. Jamie pays with cash and adds a little tip. For some reason, Susan had suggested taking a taxi, though they could have walked from the station which was literally only moments away. There are lights in all the windows of the house, and the curtains, Jamie notices, the net curtains, flicker. There's a short wall at the front on which there is a smallish hand-painted sign saying, 'Beware of the Dog'. Susan, having put on a bit of lipstick, smiles at him, then at the house. The road is a cul-de-sac of 1960s semi-detached houses. Jamie looks down the road and realises that from a particular angle, the precision of all the roofs looks like an art installation. German Expressionism. Perspective, that, he thinks. As he looks more closely, he realises that in the upstairs window of each house, someone, a child perhaps, stares out, unmoving. He calls to Susan, to point it out to her, but she's half way down the path and doesn't seem to hear him, and when he gets his phone out to take a quick snap to show her later, he can't seem to get it to work, it won't switch on. He think he must have used up all the battery and plans to charge it up later.

Susan's mother, wearing an apron, is at the door.

'I've got my key,' Susan says, and she laughs and

rattles them as if she's just won them in a competition.

Jamie stands on the tarmac drive leaning the suitcases against his legs as the women hug on the doorstep. He realises how alike they are, Susan and her mother, even on first glimpse like that. When he looks up at the upstairs window of the house, no-one is there, no child looking out, and he thinks he might have just imagined things and perhaps it's the long journey making him more tired than he realises.

Susan's mother's eyes are closed for what seems like a long time, and her hands are bony, maybe slightly arthritic, clutching the shoulder blades of her daughter. Jamie coughs. Not because he wants to attract attention, particularly, but because the air is a bit thick and smoky what with them being so close to the station. Susan's mother's eyes, when they open are fogged with something, tears or cataracts, or both. 'Oh,' she says, as if she wasn't expecting to see anyone but her daughter. 'Come on in.'

Inside, the hallway is made up almost entirely of stairs and the smell of roasting meat. 'Lush,' Susan says, when she smells it and her mother looks as if the very word has unlocked something in her.

The carpet feels a bit thin under Jamie's feet and the swirling pattern reminds him of science fiction films he's seen as a child, or in episodes of *Doctor Who*. Susan's mother leads them into the lounge, which is a through-room at the end of which is a dining table, not set. Jamie struggles a bit with the suitcases and doesn't notice, at first, that someone, a man, is sitting in one of the armchairs.

'Dad,' Susan says, and goes over to him and reaches for his hand as if to pull him to a standing position. Jamie notices that this man, Susan's dad, doesn't move. In fact, he stays sitting, as if he's a fixed point in the room, as if seated on a horse, perhaps, his legs splayed with a sense that something might be amiss, orthopaedically.

'Dad,' Susan says again. 'This is Jamie.'

Jamie steps forward, a bit self-conscious, and extends his hand. Susan's dad looks at him and there is a sense of something, like radio waves emitting. Jamie immediately notices the pockmarked skin on Susan's dad's face, like something vibrating just under the surface. Acne, he thinks, surely. Susan's dad's eyes shimmer, unfocused.

'James,' he says.

'Jamie,' Jamie says.

Susan's mother says something about taking coats and looks benignly at the suitcases blocking the doorway. When Jamie scoots them out of the way, she scurries out saying something about checking the food then appears again carrying plates.

Susan has sat down on the sofa and Jamie notices she's moved a cushion so that there's room for him, so he sits down next to her. The gas fire shoots a bluish flame as he does.

'How are you, Dad?' Susan says. She's sitting forward in this way she sometimes does, her body arched as if ready to pounce.

Her dad has a jumper on with a brown stain, a drip of something, soup or gravy or something, down the front. It's a big jumper, misshapen by frequent wear or over-washing. It makes him look like he's shrunk. He looks out beyond the back of their heads at the feature wall there, and nods.

'Your mother's cooked,' he says.

'I've cooked,' Susan's mother says, as she sets out the plates and cutlery on the dining table.

True enough, the smell of cooking is strong and rich, hanging around in the air, almost visibly so. Jamie suspects it's roast beef or pork, something animal-based, and he shuffles a bit in his seat.

'There's enough for everyone,' Susan's mother says, brightly. 'Don't move yet.' And she disappears, or seems to.

There's a kind of gap, a void, that happens, with only the hiss of the gas fire filling it, and Susan smiles, looking around the place, then says, 'Jamie's just finished his PhD.'

'Nearly,' Jamie says. 'I've still got the viva to do.'

Susan's dad heaves a sigh and seems to shake his head, his eyes trained on Jamie's hand, which is holding Susan's. 'Think you're clever, do you?' he says.

There's a clock, a carriage clock, gold coloured, on the mantelpiece that has four balls visibly twirling clockwise, then anticlockwise, and the minute hand clicks, quite loudly to the hour.

'Ready,' Susan's mother calls, and Susan and Jamie stand up, quickly. Susan's dad shuffles to the edge of his seat and pivots himself up, unfolding into a standing position, grunting, placing his hand on the small of his back. Jamie motions to him to go ahead, but he ignores it, and lets Jamie go first.

The table is covered with a red tablecloth and placemats with pictures of vintage cars. Three of the plates match. Jamie takes the place with the odd plate, and the chair wobbles as he sits. When he looks down, he can see one of the legs is slightly skewiff. Something about the fixing at the seat end isn't tight enough. Susan's dad seems to notice him adjusting the way he sits, and shakes his head.

Susan's mother brings in a baking tray using oven gloves, and places it in the centre of the table. Jamie is right, it's meat, the carcass's steam wafts a heavy, salty smell. It still sizzles in its own fat. It still looks like part of a live creature to Jamie – not a leg, more than that. Out of the corner of his eye, Jamie sees, or maybe he just feels, Susan look at him. Susan's mother brings in dishes of peas and roast potatoes. Susan's dad, who hasn't yet sat down, starts sharpening the carving knife with the honing steel. He seems to perform the process as a kind of art form, as an interpretive dance. Watching him is like watching a magician about to produce a bunch of flowers or a rabbit from nowhere. Jamie feels the knife come perilously close to his head but is afraid of moving too much because of the chair, and the loose leg.

Eventually, Susan's dad stops sharpening the knife, and begins carving the meat. Jamie watches as the knife saws through the flesh, and blood seeps through as if from a fresh wound.

'Ladies first,' Susan's dad says, placing the first slice on Susan's plate. 'Gentlemen second.' And he places the next slice onto his own plate.

Susan's mother says, 'Yum.'

Susan picks up the dish of peas and looks at Jamie. She spoons some onto his plate.

Susan's dad delivers slices of meat to Susan's mother's plate, and then on top of Jamie's peas.

'Who put the "Pea" in PhD, James, old son?' he says, and Susan laughs and nudges Jamie's arm with her elbow. When he looks at her, there's lipstick on her front tooth and he wants to tell her, but doesn't. The table seems to rattle, the cutlery; and the tray of meat seems to stir as if, to Jamie, it might awaken, unfurl itself and escape.

'Vibrations from the train,' Susan says, and places her hand on the table as if to steady it. Susan's dad picks up an entire slice of meat with his fork and slowly brings it to his mouth, saying, 'Late' or 'Eat.'

Jamie watches as Susan and her parents cut up the meat on their plates, and eat, hungrily. There is gravy or juice or something running down Susan's mother's chin and she doesn't wipe it away. His own plate of food remains untouched. To attract Susan's attention, Jamie rests his hand very gently on her thigh. She turns to him and says, 'Lush,' then returns to eating her food. Susan's dad notices and with his mouth full, says, 'Is he always like this?' And he turns to Jamie and says, 'Are you?'

The table rattles again, worse this time, and a couple of peas - four or five - roll off Jamie's plate onto the red table-cloth. He's not sure whether to hold onto the table, or his chair, which is also vibrating because of the passing train. When he looks down, he sees the fixing is even looser, and the chair leg has moved to a strange, acute angle. He raises himself slightly so as to take some weight off, and feels the muscles in his legs tense and begin to tremble almost straight away.

Susan has almost finished her meal, and whilst he has been fretting about the chair, she has begun cutting up the meat on his plate. She's having to work at it because she's cutting against the grain, and her knife isn't all that sharp. Still, she pins it down with her fork and saws at it until there are several bitesize pieces. To him, it looks like a child's meal, cut up like that. Jamie watches as Susan lifts the forkful of food towards his mouth. The meat drips juice, or blood, down onto his thigh - still trembling because of the way he has to sit - and he watches it advance closer and closer still. Susan sits forward, in that way she sometimes does, her mouth open in a wide expectant O. Behind her, Susan's mother's mouth is also open. Out of the corner of his eye, he can see Susan's dad's lips forming the exact same shape. To Jamie, they suddenly look like their open mouths are the only possible openings they have, the only possible way in. And it's a reaction, maybe unconscious, maybe just an emulation, when he opens his mouth like that, and he feels, rather than tastes the meat on his tongue, and he chews it, and his whole body is trembling, not just his legs. And Susan smiles at him again, her lipstick completely worn away, and she says, 'Lush,' and, once he's swallowed, he plans to say it back.

GREGORY NORMINTON

A PRIVATE TUTOR

IN THE BASEMENT under the basement, the private
tutor swims her forty lengths. At each end she flips over and,
momentarily foetal, pushes herself off the wall. She glides
under the surface, then resumes her breaststroke. Vadim
watches her on the monitor, palms pressed against his thighs.
He knows her hours of leisure: they are pinned to the wall of
his windowless room on the fifth floor. He reminds himself to
scan the other screens but there's nothing of interest: Paulina
in the kitchen preparing lunch, Gift and Adama polishing the
banisters. Out in the street, a mother is leaning on her pram
and staring at her smartphone. In the garden, not even a cat is
stirring. He cannot see into the bedrooms. The private tutor
ploughs her furrow, never changing pace, never letting up.
When she emerges, she ignores the steps and pulls herself up
from the shallow end. She is skinny but her legs are long and
he watches them as she walks out of the frame. Vadim's eyes
travel to the corridor of the changing room. Her hips sway.
She is trailing wetness, pulling her fingers through her hair,
and he sees that she does not shave her armpits. He dislikes
this. A woman should take care with her appearance. She
never knows who might be watching.

The private tutor is employed five days a week. Her chief responsibility is for the education of Stan, who is sixteen and has other ideas. Stan used to attend one of the more prestigious public schools, which, having a new sports hall to fund, had tried hard to accommodate him. For the most part Stan submits to lessons, and the private tutor attempts to plant seeds of understanding in him. Her employer insists on receiving reports of Stan's progress, but there are limits to the candour possible. Only Artem is allowed to call his son lazy, rude, a good-for-nothing. The man has a disarming capacity for honesty, when it suits him. The other part of the private tutor's duties involves helping Stan's sister, Dasha, with her homework. In a corner of her high-ceilinged bedroom, Dasha has a cotton tepee. It has a pattern of pink hearts around it. Nobody is allowed inside the tepee except for Dasha and Anastasia her mother and the private tutor. The private tutor begins her day by walking Dasha to her school. Dasha is seven years old. She likes to hold the private tutor's hand. The private tutor reassures her about the day ahead, and tells her how much she looks forward to coming to collect her at the end of the school day. When that time comes and they get back to the big house, Dasha changes into home clothes and Paulina brings a snack up to the playroom. The private tutor supervises Dasha's homework. There isn't much of it, mostly spelling and times tables, but Dasha is determined to work hard so that she can show the fruits of her efforts to her mother. At present, Dasha's mother is away. Last month it was Manhattan, currently it's Paris. In March she will be in Monaco. Anastasia needs time off, for, as she tells Dasha when

Dasha demands attention, she suffers from brutal headaches. Artem, too, is away a great deal, on the yacht, where he does much of his business and to which on two occasions, his face glazed with the sweat of drunkenness, he has invited the private tutor. Some days, when both parents are away, Stan plays truant and hangs out with his older friends who like to show off their sports cars on the streets of central London. On these occasions, the staff are left to wander the big house, feeling strangely weightless in so much empty space.

Nessa returns each evening to her one-bedroom ground-floor flat in Earlsfield. It's a subdivided semi, a quarter of a home. Dust from the busy road spills under the door and smears the barred windows. Her mother's cat, entrusted to Nessa so that she might have company, tries to stir itself from its basket. Arthritic, it moves like faulty clockwork between two rooms. At night she finds large slugs, like suppurating turds, feeding on the cat's food. She suffocates the slugs in plastic bags and throws these in the bin, but more appear within days. The cat seems not to notice, or else it's inured to the competition. Nessa makes time each evening to stroke the cat. It butts its head against her. Its purr is intermittent like an engine with parts coming loose. She no longer sets it on the corner of her bed at night because it is becoming incontinent and has twice failed to reach its litter tray on time. One evening she returns from Knightsbridge to find her mother's cat cold and stiffening on its cushion. She telephones her mother, who lives with her second husband on the Dorset coast, to tell her what has happened. She tells her mother that she is fine. She hangs up, then wraps the cat and its basket and its food and water bowls and its medicine and its food sachets into a large bin bag that she carries out into the street. There is a skip five houses down full of broken insulation boards and now it also contains a dead cat. Nessa returns to the flat, puts on the TV and works her way through a bottle of Tesco Sauvignon Blanc.

The private tutor sits in the back of the second Range Rover at the pheasant shoot in Hampshire. Stan will have his physics lesson when he and his father take a break from the shooting. Artem is a good shot. He told her this several times on the drive down. He likes to travel to the Cairngorms to shoot grouse in an estate right next door to the Queen's. He does all the things an English country gentleman does, ordering his checked shirts from Farlows, his tweed breeks and fleeces from Campbells of Beauly. Last year he flew to Botswana to shoot some very big game. Stan is eager to do the same. The private tutor reads through her lesson plan. Lunch for the guns will be in half an hour. Paulina has prepared her a sandwich. The private tutor gazes out the window. A line of men is walking up the birds through the field. The guns lean back and fire. She watches the pheasants fold in the air. First the upwards rush, then the burst plummet. Artem tells her she should come to see his gunsmith. He would fit her easily. Everyone begins as a novice but she, Artem has noticed, has a steady hand. He would like to teach her one day.

When she's not working or entertaining Dasha, the private tutor spends time in the 'hidden house' with the servants, listening to Paulina's stories about her grandchildren in Quito, hearing Adama tell Gift how to make her life right with the Lord even as Gift boasts about her latest boyfriend. Sometimes Vadim comes in to raid the fridge and then the chatter dies. He looks Gift over and when he is gone everyone gets back to work, sliding off shared glances. Sometimes when the servants gather they gossip. They whisper about Artem's mistress, Anastasia's bulimia, Stan's stained sheets. The private tutor adds nothing to the conversation. She will say only that Stan is a reluctant pupil. Everyone agrees that Dasha is a darling. But for how much longer, Adama wonders. The private tutor excuses herself. She has another English lesson to prepare. In *Macbeth*, Birnam Wood is on the move. So is Stan. Ten minutes into the lesson, he yawns and leaves the room without explanation. The private tutor waits ten minutes for him to return from the loo, or wherever he's gone, but Stan has left the house by the time she decides to go looking for him. Three days later, when she is able to tell Artem about his son's behaviour, Artem threatens to beat the boy, but without passion, as if he too would have walked away from a lesson that bored him.

When Artem is in residence, the big house is a hive of activity. Motorcycle couriers congregate under the portico. Visitors knock at the door, show their faces to the monitor, get buzzed in and in some cases patted down. The private tutor, who has permission to move about the house if she needs to, sometimes finds herself in the atrium when guests arrive, portly gentlemen in suits, or tall women with long waxed legs and practised, languorous gestures. Some of the columnists and politicians look familiar. Here is the posh English lawyer, there the bright young things from Artem's favourite think tank. The private tutor makes haste to get away. Upstairs, she and Dasha form their own little world. It's made of bits of paper with faces and mysterious codes scribbled on them. It's made of fidget toys and Lego characters who've swapped heads and hairdos, of notepads and music boxes. On the periphery of this world sit cuddly toys and animated dolls that were brought back from Harrods. These Dasha plays with only occasionally. Her enthusiasm for each burns out quickly and she returns to her inventions, narrating her play to Nessa, who unlike everyone else in the big house does not seem to run out of patience with her. Nessa and Dasha sometimes comb the hair of Dasha's oldest and least elegant dolls, and sometimes Nessa combs Dasha's hair, which is long and black and opens like a veil of silk when Nessa sifts it with her fingers. Dasha makes cards for her friends at school and Nessa cuts complex patterns out of crepe paper for Dasha to glue on. Nessa reads old-fashioned books about old-fashioned children who have never seen a smartphone or begged for an iPad. Nessa and Dasha. They sound, Nessa says, like two of Santa's reindeers. Dasha laughs, displaying the gaps between her new and overlarge teeth. Stan, in his bedroom across the landing, hears none of this, immersed in the slaughter of *Call of Duty*.

Nessa.
　Hm?
　A boy at school is mean to me.
　What does he do?
　He takes my pens and hides them.
　Why does he do that?
　I don't know.
　You should give him a kick up the bum.
　I *can't*.
　Tell the teacher. That's what she's there for. Do you get your pens back?

He tells me to look for them.

Maybe he's trying to get your attention.

He tells everyone I'm stupid.

But you're not. You're clever, and what's more important, unlike that silly boy, you're kind.

You said I should kick him up the bum.

I didn't mean it.

I'd like to set my Papa on him.

Listen, Dasha. If he does it again, you tell me first.

What will you do?

I'll put a spell on him. His nose will double in size and his willy will drop off. There. It doesn't seem so terrible when you picture that happening to him.

I wish you *were* a witch.

Perhaps I am.

A good one.

All witches are good, it's just men who pretend otherwise.

In a hut in the woods.

Making spells and potions.

But not like Baba Yaga. She eats people.

Nothing like Baba Yaga. Mind you, a hut on chicken legs would be handy. You could live anywhere you like. Just hold on to the furniture and off you go.

I'd come with you.

Of course you would.

We'd be happy together. Nessa?

Yes?

It's just a story, isn't it?

Yes. It's just a story.

Nessa speaks to few people when she's at home. Her mother,

sometimes her mother's husband when he gets to the phone first. Once or twice a month, her oldest friend calls for what she calls a catch-up. Anouk and Nessa were at school together, then at university. Anouk lives in Nottingham where she works as a solicitor. She's married to another solicitor, with a baby on the way. It was Anouk who'd suggested private tutor work, having taken some on herself after graduating. Silly pay, she'd said, especially with foreigners if you play the Oxford graduate routine. You hate your job, Anouk had said, why not chuck it in, whore yourself to one of the big houses in Mayfair? Nessa had written down the details of the agency. This was how, after a stint with a Nigerian oil baron whose wayward daughter narrowly passed her A-levels, Nessa had ended up as private tutor to Artem's and Anastasia's children. Anouk often asks after them, eager for gossip and anecdote, but tonight, when her friend calls, Nessa doesn't pick up. She sits watching her reflection in the television's mirror. The hot chocolate on her lap forms a milk skin. The phone buzzes on the arm of her chair. She gets slowly to her feet and turns off the phone. In the bedroom her duvet is turned down in one corner. As her mother used to leave it when Nessa was a child.

Vadim watches the private tutor swimming her lengths. It is typically generous of Artem to allow it. The cook and the cleaning women don't get to use the pool, which is a shame as he wouldn't mind seeing Gift in a bikini. Perhaps it wouldn't occur to them to ask. Or perhaps a private tutor is a higher servant than a cook or a cleaning maid. Vadim wishes he could zoom in. The private tutor, he has noticed, takes no time to rest between lengths. She never luxuriates in the experience of water. Artem calls her the 'Ice Queen'. A stuck-up bitch,

Vadim reckons, what people here call a real cold fish. But Artem says no, she's English, the emotions are buried deep. Vadim would like to delve deep into the Ice Queen to extract them. She avoids his gaze because she knows this. Women always do, even the frigid ones. Anastasia is the exception. Vadim does not look at her and she does not look at him. They might as well be different species. It's always easier when Anastasia is away. When she returns from her trips, his boss's mood takes a turn for the worse. Vadim has overheard their rows, is familiar with the routine. When Artem has been spending too much time with his whores, Anastasia demands reassurance, affection, and when these aren't forthcoming she settles on demands for more money. And Artem laughs. What money? He's a poor man, he's not the beneficial owner of *any* of his properties in Britain. He has obligations abroad. Finally, one of his women will chose a necklace and he will offer it to Anastasia, often on the yacht, and there will be a night of matrimonial fucking. Vadim wonders what the boss's wife is like in the sack, and this makes him return to the board of monitors. The private tutor has stepped out of the pool. Unseen by him, she has made it to the changing room. This puts Vadim in a temper. He watches the last echoes of her movements across the empty swimming pool.

The referendum is four weeks away and there are important visitors to the big house. The private tutor remains on the fifth floor with Stan and Dasha. They can hear the booming voices, the loud laughter downstairs as the visitors are ushered into Artem's private rooms. Nessa has entered those rooms on three occasions, at Artem's invitation, to discuss the progress of her pupils and decline the offer of a drink. There's a library full of venerable books with ornate bindings, a job lot, Artem told her, from a Scots baronial pile. There's an office with Louis XV furniture and an oak desk to rival the one in the Oval Office. Between these there runs a corridor with framed photographs of film stars and celebrity authors who've attended Artem's garden parties. Lastly, there is what Artem calls his recreation room, which the private tutor has not seen but which contains, according to Stan, who needs to boast of access to his father, a Peloton bike and a massage table, a drinks cabinet stowed in a seventeenth-century globe of the heavens, a wall-sized TV and several large leather sofas where Artem and his friends kick back and drink Japanese beer. The private tutor persuades Stan to knuckle down to his English lesson, but Stan sits beside her grudgingly, resentment in his hunched-up shoulders. He wants to be downstairs with the men. He wants to learn from his father how to be powerful in this world, and he doubts reading Shakespeare's tragedies can help him. Quietly the private tutor responds. On the contrary, she says. On the contrary.

Can I come in?

You can but nobody else.

Oh, you've made it cosy in here. How's Pug?

He's Pinkie.

I thought he was Pug.

Pinkie Pug. He has a cold and that's why the cushion's all snotty.

Ugh. Poor Pinkie. I've got a tissue for him.

He doesn't know how to blow his nose, he's only a dog.

I like the fairy lights, did you move them from over your bed? And who's this?

She's new.

What's her name?

Nessa Doll.

Oh.

Mama bought her in Dubai. She looks like you, only she doesn't wear glasses. They'd make her look clever.

Do you think my glasses make me look clever?

But she doesn't need them because she's a doll. Do you want to hold her?

Nessa Doll.

She's going to sleep in my bed tonight because she doesn't know anybody yet.

I think that's very thoughtful of you.

She closes her eyes when you tip her over. Stan says she's a spooky doll but she isn't.

Of course she isn't.

Mama bought him a Rolex.

He showed it to me.

He's already got one.

Well. It can be useful to have a spare.

I only get cheap presents.

Nessa Doll is a much better present than some chunky watch. Your mother loves you, you know that, don't you?

She never comes in the tent. She doesn't want to mess up her hair.

Well. That's what comes of having an expensive hair-do. You have a crow's nest like mine, you can crawl into as many tents as you please. Do you want a hug?

And Nessa Doll.

And Nessa Doll.

The half-term holidays, and Stan is off with friends, sleeping at their houses, sitting in their cars. The private tutor has accepted Anastasia's request that she work as babysitter for the duration. Each morning she greets Dasha with the promise of an outing. This is new. Until now, Artem has never allowed her to take Dasha on daytrips. But he has been summoned to Moscow, so he gives her cash to spend and presses his hand over her fist, his breath smelling of coffee and vodka. Take your phone, he says. And so Nessa and Dasha step out into warm sunshine and take taxis – Artem refuses to countenance public transport – to the London Eye and the National Gallery, to the Natural History Museum, where they stare into the jaws of the animatronic T-Rex, to London Zoo and the V&A. Dasha comes home with fact books on art and nature, with lift-the-flap histories that allow her to peep into the Coliseum and a Pharaoh's tomb, with butterfly cages and portable microscopes through which she inspects the wings of a fly, the eye of a spider, a sporophyte plucked from a crust of moss. All of these discoveries Dasha shares with her mother, who, suddenly zealous, insists on bathing her daughter and doing the evening routine. Nessa walks off into the London evening. Nobody pays attention to her as she visits different cash machines. Nobody pays attention as she stocks up on sachets of soup and energy bars, on dried fruit and plasters, Calpol and toothpaste. There is nothing remarkable about a woman buying a cheap phone from a kiosk outside a Tube station. Nessa gets home and lays out her purchases on her bed. On the Saturday, she takes the train to visit her mother in Dorset. It's the first time she has gone there all year.

For two days, a pair of large, wheeled suitcases has stood

upright in the narrow hallway of Nessa's flat. Nessa has to squeeze sideways to pass them on her way to work. In the big house, Stan has holed himself up in the cinema in the basement. Artem is abroad and the private tutor knocks on the door of Anastasia's second bedroom, the one she occupies when her husband is away and sometimes when he's at home. A sleep-furred voice within mutters that she, the private tutor, can manage perfectly well on her own. Stan however refuses to leave the basement and she has neither the strength nor the licence to force him. She retreats to the kitchen and sits, in near silence, with Paulina, who is worrying about one of her nephews who has got into trouble with the police. When Vadim bursts into the kitchen demanding to know why she, the private tutor, is not at work, she tells him to fuck off. This is not well received, but what can Vadim do save make a note for when the boss returns? Paulina stares at the private tutor. Later, she will tell Gift and Adama, and the gardeners who are preparing the garden for the referendum-night party.

Nessa stands at the foot of her bed, her gaze moving between the paper in her hand and the items laid out on the duvet. Having checked her inventory, she packs the items into a large rucksack. The rucksack travelled with her, back in the day, to South America and the Mediterranean. It's worn yet sturdy and every inch of its capacity is put to use. When she has finished packing the rucksack and given every cord a knuckle-whitening tug, Nessa sits on the corner of the bed where her mother's cat used to sleep. She extracts the SIM card from her smartphone. She contemplates it for a minute, then takes it for a stroll.

❧

The next day, Stan continues in his state of revolt. This time he refuses to emerge from his bedroom and its noise of artillery fire. Artem isn't back yet and Anastasia has left for a spa break in Worcestershire. When Vadim comes to investigate the gathering of staff on the fourth floor, he shrugs at the impasse. If he had instructions he would, he says, cheerfully pull Konstantin out by the ear. But in the absence of directions from above . . . The private tutor averts not just her gaze but her face from him. He passes her closely and makes a show of sniffing the air. When she leaves the big house minutes later, he watches her receding figure until it vanishes from the screen.

Later the same day, Nessa arrives early at the school gates. The waiting mums and nannies pay her little attention, she could be one of them, somewhat scruffy, a rich bohemian. The children emerge and Dasha wears her cardigan on one arm, she drags her Totoro rucksack, her face is a fraught with emotion. She buries herself in Nessa's embrace. Nessa kneels and wipes the hot tears from Dasha's face. She places her fingertips on the child's forehead, kisses her there. It takes Nessa several minutes to calm her, and then, hiccupping with sorrow, Dasha clings to her hand all the way home. Paulina glares with concern when she brings a plate of kiwi slices to Dasha's bedroom. She's exhausted, the private tutor says. There's a mean boy at school who bullies her. Dasha says that she wants her mama. Paulina tells her what she already knows, that her mother is away for a few days, and this makes Dasha howl again. She pushes the plate of fruit away from her, then kicks at it when it doesn't go far enough. It's all right, the private tutor says, picking up the kiwi slices. Paulina reaches to touch the child's hair, draws back her fingers. She promises to put extra marshmallows in Dasha's hot chocolate. Once again, Gift and Adama have been drawn away from their duties, they stand in the doorway watching. She'll be fine, the private tutor tells them. Leave it to me.

The weekend before the referendum and Nessa and Dasha are on another outing. They sit next to each other on a northbound train. They have not taken a table, so Dasha's magazine and plastic freebies are arranged on the pull-down tray. Dasha's eyes shimmer as she watches the countryside race past. Nessa has bought her a chocolate rabbit. The tickets she paid for with cash taken out in Camden a week ago. Dasha bites into the rabbit's conjoined ears. She offers Nessa a spit-sheened fragment. It's yours, says Nessa, and she touches Dasha's head, then looks up the aisle. Their bags are stuffed into the overloaded storage shelves. Dasha's Totoro rucksack is distinctive. Every so often she asks why they have to keep it in a Tesco bag-for-life. Dasha asks where they are going and when will they get there and Nessa says, to a very special place. Will there be toys and a TV? There will be everything, Nessa whispers, that a little girl could ever want.

When Papa gets back from his boat, will he come and join us?
  I expect so.
  And Mama will come too?
  Have a crisp.
  I don't like those. Too salty. Where's *your* papa?
  He left when I was your age.
  Where did he go?
  Australia.

Have you been to Australia? I have.

I know.

I didn't see your papa though.

He was probably hiding. That's what he does.

But you kept your mama.

And she drummed into me the need to work hard, to get good grades, so I could support myself.

Is that where we're going, to the seaside?

We're going to the woods. To a very special place that belonged to my grandparents. I spent my summers there. I was happy and so will we be.

Are the woods spooky?

Of course not.

Are there wolves?

No. Squirrels though. Red ones, not like London squirrels. And golden eagles. And deer, great big stags with antlers.

Just so long as Mama . . .

I can't hear you.

So long as Mama comes.

I'll be with you. That's nice, isn't it?

Yeah.

Every hour of every day. We'll sleep in the same big bed, and I'll read you stories. We'll cook sausages on a campfire and watch the stars, real stars, a whole sky of them like you've never seen. Have you ever travelled in space, Dasha? Where we're going, you can dive straight into it. There's nothing to stop you seeing forever.

Dasha is lying asleep across both seats when the train terminates at Aberdeen. None of the other passengers with whom they shared the compartment hours ago has made it this far.

Nessa, who has been watching from the other side of the aisle, gently tugs Dasha's earlobe to wake her without a start. Dasha stands dazed and open mouthed while Nessa wrestles with the luggage. Even though it's a warm evening, Dasha must, like Nessa, put on her new baseball cap before they step down to the platform. She clings to the cold metal arm of one of the wheeled suitcases. Not far to go now, says Nessa. She hails a taxi at the rank and refuses the cabbie's offer of help with their luggage. The inside of the taxi smells of peppermints and dog fur. Dasha watches a grey city in golden evening light, then wide fields, hills, settlements of white bungalows, finally a landscape of pines and birch and pastures thick with rushes. Nessa says loudly, in the American accent she's been putting on with people all day, that this is good, they can go from here. The cabbie, whose big peppery moustache Dasha thinks must fill with soup when he eats, watches them in the rear-view mirror. Really, says Nessa, drop us off here. So he does, and takes the cash, and his tyres splash in puddles as he reverses down the lane. Nessa squeezes Dasha's hand. They walk on into the woods. Dasha is weary, dragging her toes as they negotiate a dirt track. Nessa pants under the weight of her rucksack, one suitcase to each hand. Irritable, exhausted, they contemplate the footpath, scarcely visible through heather, that leads to the bothy.

The bothy is one room with a stove and a sink under a single-glazed window. The hessian floor is littered with dead bees. Two sofas face a dusty coffee table. There's a low bookcase with old hardbacks and faded OS maps, and a stepladder leads to a mezzanine almost entirely taken up with a double mattress. The loo, Dasha is appalled to discover, is a bucket outside shielded from the elements by corrugated metal sheets and a tarpaulin. Nessa produces Scotch eggs and samosas and two small cartons of apple juice. When they've eaten, she settles Dasha on one of the sofas and covers her in a blanket shaken loose from the rucksack. Sleep, says Nessa, and when you wake up you'll be in a fairy tale. Exhaustion relieves Dasha of her discomfort, she moans, cries a little, and when she stirs the light in the world has altered. Nessa is asleep on the other sofa. The dust and the dead bees have gone. There are packets of cereal and tea and rice arrayed on the windowsill. Her toys and her drawing paper sit on the coffee table in the shade of a vase filled with scruffy flowers. Dasha climbs the stepladder to discover a bed with two sleeping bags laid across it and her clothes neatly folded under the sloping ceiling. She climbs down the stepladder, contemplates Nessa asleep on the sofa. Nessa opens her eyes. Welcome home, she says.

The fine weather holds and in the shelter of the hills the woods are warm and resin scented. Nessa and Dasha clear some of the overgrown beds near the bothy and dig over the soil. Nessa places sunflower seeds in Dasha's cupped hands and Dasha plants them gingerly, until she loses her fear of dirt and begins to wear it like a fashion statement. The bothy's water comes sweet and peat-stained from a well in the birches, and they begin each day with the ritual of dipping and raising the plastic bucket. Nessa cooks eggs and bacon on the stove. When these run out, they walk for twenty minutes to a tiny village with only one shop. Nessa becomes American again and Dasha must wait outside looking busy, though how she's meant to do this she never discovers. The front pages of the newspapers are loud with news. Nessa emerges from the shop and tells Dasha the result of the referendum. Is that good, Dasha asks. It makes no difference to us, says Nessa, but she is quieter than usual on the walk back. Along the footpath bird cherries are in flower. Aspen quake with their song of rain. Dasha collects feathery tufts of glittering root-moss and picks a sort of salad from the bark of an oak that Nessa calls lungwort. The days pass. They go for long hikes, with picnics, and Dasha looks for the crested tits and Scottish crossbills that Nessa showed her in a book. On very still days, Dasha steps outside to feel a tremulous mask settle on her face. Then comes the itching, the crawling in her scalp and the run back to shelter. Most days, however, a breeze keeps the midges at bay. Some evenings they make a campfire and melt marsh-mallows in the flames, or bake white dough knotted about the ends of sticks. Things my grandfather taught me, Nessa says. Dasha's grandfather lives in Miami. She doubts he would know what to do in the wild. Because summer comes late this far north, the sun works overtime to make up the difference. This is why Dasha goes to bed and gets up in daylight. Only once does Nessa wake her when she climbs the stepladder to her sleeping bag. Dasha is aware of near darkness, a low blue haze in the long window. There's no sound of traffic. There are no planes. She asks, in a croaky voice, if Nessa could read her a little more from *Swallows and Amazons*. There are lots of books for children in the bothy. My grandma read them to me, says Nessa. And now it's you, says Dasha. And now it's me.

They are bedding in. Nessa heats water on the stove and they have shallow, shivery baths in an old metal tub. Washing isn't much fun so they don't do it often. Their clothes begin to smell musty. Outside, tiny green heads emerge in the flowerbed. Dasha befriends a lichen-shaggy oak and learns to climb it, sitting with pendulous legs in a fork high up. She goes to the latrine without needing Nessa to wait for her on the other side of the tarpaulin. Each becomes accustomed to the other's snoring or farting, or rustling in her sleeping bag. But Dasha starts waking up long before Nessa. Then she frets. She imagines scenarios and buries her head under her sleeping bag, into the heat and smell of her body. Like a mole seeking refuge in its burrow.

The early summer warmth continues and the water level drops in the well. Dasha misses TV. She misses Lego construction videos on YouTube. She asks after her mother and is plunged into the terrible loneliness of Nessa's disappointment. Isn't Dasha happy? Dasha promises that she is and Nessa takes them on another walk. In the evening they make a fire but Dasha is losing her appetite for scorched marshmallows and campfire bread. Nessa insists on hikes through the forest, though they must avoid the open moors and major footpaths, so that heather and blaeberry catch at Dasha's boots. They are far from the bothy when the midges descend and Dasha sits on a rock, slapping at her face. She wants to speak to her mama. She wants to borrow Nessa's phone, even if it is rubbish and can't connect to the internet. No, says Nessa. Why not? Because there's no reception. Why? Because they're here, Nessa says, to get away from all that shit.

Dasha comes in, covered in twigs and shreds of lichen, from climbing her oak, to find Nessa kneeling in front of the coffee table, counting ten-pound notes. Dasha says that it looks like a lot. It isn't, says Nessa. The tins and cartons of food are dwindling. When they go now to the little village shop, Dasha asks for chocolate and treats, but Nessa shakes her head and sends her to wait in the bus shelter. Why can't Dasha go into the shop with her? She wants to look at the magazines. No, says Nessa. But she's *bored*, why does she have to wait in the boring bus shelter? Because I say so, says Nessa, and she leans forward as if to hug Dasha, but it isn't that, though Dasha is ready for it, a consoling gesture to make up for the hardness in her voice, it isn't a hug but it's a push, Nessa pushes her towards the bus shelter and it's so sudden and unprecedented that Dasha staggers. She manages to keep herself from falling and looks up to see Nessa's back as she enters the shop. Dasha is a good girl, she waits in the bus shelter, but she can't keep the tears from falling. Nessa returns with cheap sausages and potatoes and eggs that aren't even free range. They have, she says, almost no fruit. She appears enraged by this, and Dasha must hurry to catch up as Nessa strides with the rucksack on her back. Dasha wants to be forgiven. She wants to hold Nessa's hand. She wants to push her into the heather and run back to the shop.

Vadim inserts the coffee cup in the holder and checks that it's firmly wedged. He doesn't want to stain the upholstery. He sits at the steering wheel, feeling the bulk of the car around him. He rests his eyes on the flow of traffic. Not for the first time today, he wishes he were still a smoker. But he is a man of iron will. Artem knows this, it's why he was admitted into the family circle from the very beginning of all this, Anastasia hysterical, Artem with a face like thunder, even Stan on edge, swallowing repeatedly and swiping at his phone. What was the boy doing, who was he communicating with? Nobody must know about this, Artem said. As far as Dasha's school is concerned, we're keeping her at home with a heavy cold. This is something we can sort out between ourselves. And he looked at Vadim with many words in his eyes that Vadim understood. Perhaps she has overheard things best unheard. Something to give her leverage in a police interview room. Vadim doesn't know. He hasn't asked. He's simply glad of the chance to put his skills to use. He lifts the plastic lid from his coffee and places his left hand above the cup, enjoying the hot vapour as it forms on his palm. When he was a boy, he used to do the same with candles, testing how close he could put his skin to the flame, how long he could stand it. None of his friends had his staying power. It was how he kept calm when the family started losing its shit. Artem worst of all. He'd expected a demand for money. While they waited, Vadim used his contacts to search for electronic traces. He found nothing in her hovel of a flat - no plane tickets, no telling receipts - except, how quaint, an address book that would prove invaluable. Three days passed and Artem called another meeting. He said that profit might not be the motive. Envy? Revenge? But revenge for what, on whose behalf? She was just a crazy bitch, said Anastasia, who wants to torture a loving mother, who having no family feels the need to smear herself all over someone else's. That's too easy, Vadim thinks. She's a rational actor. Within limits. Deep down, she must know she can't get away with it. And maybe that's the point. Maybe the Ice Queen has been waiting for him all along? And now he's on his way. You must never disappoint royalty.

Dasha knows she must stop whining. She knows, because her mother has told her, that it's very ugly to complain. But the sausages are burnt and their skin is tough to cut. Nessa reaches across and cuts them up for her. The tines of her fork scrape against the plate. Why is Dasha covering her ears? It hurts, she says. Just eat, will you? But Nessa too is struggling with the food. She doesn't so much eat it as move it about on her plate. This is inedible, she says, just as Dasha has started enjoying the meat under the charring, and she takes Dasha's plate and scrapes the contents into the bin. I was eating that, yelps Dasha. She feels rage. Heartbreak. It's out of all proportion, but how can she hold it in? Her body isn't big enough. She shouts, What are we going to eat now? I'll butter some bread, says Nessa. Bread isn't a balanced meal, Dasha says. It's not even *trying.* Nessa returns to the coffee table for her own plate. This too she empties into the bin. She reaches into the bin and pulls out the bag. The bin falls with a clatter and Nessa throttles the plastic bag and carries it like a dead chicken out of the bothy. She closes the door with a bang. Dasha goes to the window above the sink. She watches Nessa with the bin bag. It's ten minutes to the municipal bins. Dasha waits, alone, hungry.

Vadim stops to refuel the Range Rover at Stirling Services. He stands with one hand on the trembling nozzle, his other hand flat against the black sheen of the tinted back window. According to the Sat Nav he will reach his destination in two hours. Assuming his intelligence is correct, and his surmise. It had been wise not to approach the private tutor's mother. She might have raised the alarm, assuming she's in contact. Much easier to fall into conversation with the ugly friend in the pub, Anouk, very indiscreet and guileless. Hey, they had a mutual friend! What were the chances? He'd soon learned about the student holidays in the tiny cottage in Scotland. Shitting in a bucket. Long walks and getting rat-arsed on cheap wine and whisky. It won't be such a party when he gets there. The more he thinks about it, the more he likes his theory that her escapade, rather than being a cry for help, as the phone-ins call it, is an attempt at self-destruction. She always was the moody, self-obsessed type. And yet it's hard to tell what goes on in another person's head. All we have is the surface. It's almost nothing to go on. He shakes the nozzle of the pump. Like shaking the last drops out of your dick. He enjoys the sound and sensation of returning the nozzle to its cradle. He goes to pay for his fuel. Whatever it's all been about, it will soon be over.

Dasha. That was mean of me. I shouldn't have left you alone. But you knew I was coming back, didn't you? You know I'd never abandon you. It's just that sometimes. Please. Dasha. I know it's been difficult the last couple of days. I have a lot on my mind and sometimes that makes me less kind than I want to be. Because it's all about kindness. Do you understand? It's about, just once, just someone, putting themselves second. You see, there's a gap in life, and people are always trying to fill it, but they fill it with the wrong things. So they reach for more and more, and the gap just keeps growing. Listen, I've known this place since I was a child. I was happy here. Because out here, in the woods, there is no gap. I'm sorry I upset you. I promise I'll never be mean to you again. Dasha. Can I have a hug? Can you forgive me? Can I have a hug?

The absence of a road is, of course, no obstacle. Vadim enjoys the whiplash from the shocked branches, the jolting off the bumps. In a minute he's arrived. It's not exactly a dacha, more a hut. He parks behind a stand of birches, keeping his eyes on the front door. There's nowhere for them to run that he can't run faster, but he's stiff from all this driving. It's important not to frighten the child. He walks towards the hut. A face appears in the window. He runs as the door opens, and now he is chasing them, the woman bustling the little girl into the trees, dragging her by the sleeve. She wants to go faster, he can see her panic, but she cannot let go of the child. He stops running. Dasha, he calls. The child squirms in the woman's arms. She tries to keep hold of her, but Dasha has seen Vadim and recognised him, she shakes herself loose and runs, as fast as her legs will carry her, into Vadim's arms. Vadim squeezes her back. Her thin shoulders. Her hair is tangled and knotted. He looks up at the private tutor and sees defeat in her face. She stands, watching. She makes no attempt to win the girl back. She makes no attempt to escape, either. Vadim takes Dasha by the hand and walks her, crooning in their own tongue, to the car. He promises her treats when they gets home. Her mother plans for them to go on holiday, just the two of them. He opens the passenger door where the booster seat is waiting. Dasha climbs into the seat and he hands her the iPad that Artem has bought for her. He has already saved Lego-building videos for her to watch. You wait there, little one, he says. I'll be back in a moment. He locks the car and walks back into the trees. The private tutor is waiting for him. And this makes sense. It's the confirmation he was looking for. He stops and lets his arms hang at his sides. Does she want to explain? She shakes her head. At the very least, does she understand what must happen now? He asked Artem about this, in a professional way, and Artem said it was up to him, but now that he has the opportunity he lacks the impulse. He doesn't want blood on his clothes. That would distress Dasha. You came, the private tutor says, not the police. Better that way, he says. You could make, she says, a citizen's arrest. Vadim shrugs. I think you want more than police. I would deserve it, she says. Because you took her? No. Not because I took her. He wades through the heather till he stands almost on her toes. She does not flinch but he senses a quickening in her breath. He considers placing his fingers on her face. There are tiny biting insects settling like a mist, making his skin prickle. He thinks, there could be hikers. He leans so close than he can smell her breath. It reeks. You will not get from me, he says, what you think you deserve. He turns about and walks to the Range Rover. There is no sound of movement in the heather behind him. He sees Dasha on the passenger seat. She looks up as he opens his door, then returns her attention to the iPad. Just as well. He gets into the driver's seat. He feels very tired. OK, he says. Let's go home.

CONTRIBUTOR
BIOGRAPHIES

ALAN BEARD has published two story collections, *Taking Doreen Out of the Sky* (Picador, 1999) and *You Don't Have to Say* (Tindal Street Press, 2010). He has had numerous stories in magazines and anthologies, most recently in *Digbeth Stories*, *Litro, Leon, trampset, Outside Left* and *Best Microfiction 2024*. He is a longstanding member of Tindal Street Fiction Group, who celebrated their fortieth anniversary in 2023.

KEVIN BONIFACE is a writer and artist from Huddersfield in West Yorkshire.

PAUL BROWNSEY is a former philosophy lecturer at Glasgow University. His first collection, *His Steadfast Love and Other Stories*, was published by Lethe Press, New Jersey, USA, and was a finalist in the Lambda Literary Awards.

CLAIRE CARROLL is a writer and PhD researcher whose work explores how experimental short fiction writing can reimagine how humans relate to the natural and non-human world. Her short stories have been published by journals including *The White Review, The London Magazine, Gutter,* 3:AM, and *Lunate,* and *Short Fiction Journal.* Her debut collection, *The Unreliable Nature Writer,* was released in June 2024 by Scratch Books.

ECM CHEUNG is a London-based, Birmingham-bred writer, filmmaker, pamphleteer and bookseller.

JONATHAN COE is the author of fifteen novels, the latest of which is *The Proof of My Innocence.*

ROSIE GARLAND writes poetry, long and short fiction, and sings with post-punk band The March Violets. Poetry collection *What Girls Do in the Dark* (Nine Arches Press) was shortlisted for the Polari Prize 2021. Her latest novel, *The Fates* (Quercus) is a retelling of the Greek myth of the Fates, and her first collection of short fiction is forthcoming with Fly On The Wall Press in January 2025. In 2023, she was made Fellow of the Royal Society of Literature, and Val McDermid has named her one of the most compelling LGBT+ writers in the UK today.

KERRY HADLEY-PRYCE has had three novels published by Salt Publishing, *The Black Country* (Michael Schmidt Prize); *Gamble* (shortlisted for the Encore Award) and *God's Country.* Her fourth novel, *Lie of the Land,* is due for publication in 2025. With a PhD in creative writing she now teaches creative writing and has contributed to Palgrave's *Smell, Memory & Literature in the Black Country* anthology. She has had short stories published in *Best British Short Stories 2023, Takahe Magazine, Fictive Dream* and *The Incubator.*

TIMOTHY J JARVIS is a writer with an interest in the antic and strange. His novel, *The Wanderer*, was first released in summer 2014 by Perfect Edge Books and republished by Zagava in 2022. Short fiction has appeared in various venues and in 2023 a collection, *Treatises on Dust*, was published by Swan River Press. He lives in Bedford.

CYNAN JONES is an acclaimed fiction writer from the west coast of Wales. His work has appeared in over twenty countries and in journals and magazines including *Granta*, *Freeman's* and the *New Yorker*. He has also written a screenplay for the hit crime drama *Hinterland*, a collection of tales for children, and a number of stories for BBC Radio. He has been longlisted and shortlisted for numerous awards and won, among other prizes, the Wales Book of the Year Fiction Prize, a Jerwood Fiction Uncovered Award and the BBC National Short Story Award.

BHANU KAPIL lives in Cambridge, where she is an Extraordinary Fellow of Churchill College. Her last book of poetry, *How To Wash A Heart*, won the TS Eliot Prize. Two new editions of *Incubation: a space for monsters* were published in 2023 by Prototype (UK) and Kelsey Street Press (USA).

SONYA MOOR writes and translates short fiction. Her work is published in literary reviews and anthologies, including *Best British Short Stories 2022*, and recognised for awards such as the Cinnamon Literature Award, Seán O'Faoláin International Short Story Competition and Bridport Short Story Prize. Her collection *The Comet and Other Stories* is published by

Cōnfingō, and her translation of Albertine Sarrazin's *The Crib and Other Stories* is upcoming from Cōnfingō. www.sonyamoor.com

ALISON MOORE's first novel, *The Lighthouse*, was shortlisted for the Man Booker Prize and the National Book Awards (New Writer of the Year), winning the McKitterick Prize. She recently published her fifth novel, *The Retreat*, and a trilogy for children, beginning with *Sunny and the Ghosts*. Her short fiction has been included in previous *Best British Short Stories* and *Best British Horror* anthologies, broadcast on BBC Radio, and collected in *The Pre-War House and Other Stories* and *Eastmouth and Other Stories*. Born in Manchester in 1971, she lives near Nottingham with her husband Dan and son Arthur.

GREGORY NORMINTON is the author of five novels and two collections of short stories. He is a Senior Lecturer in Creative Writing at Manchester Metropolitan University. He lives with his wife and daughter in Sheffield.

NICHOLAS ROYLE is the author of *Telepathy and Literature* (1990), *The Uncanny* (2003), and *Veering: A Theory of Literature* (2011), as well as books about EM Forster, Jacques Derrida, William Shakespeare and Hélène Cixous. He has also published two novels, *Quilt* (2010) and *An English Guide to Birdwatching* (2017), and a memoir, *Mother* (2020). He is co-author with Andrew Bennett of *An Introduction to Literature, Criticism and Theory* (Sixth edition, 2023) and *This Thing Called Literature* (Second edition, 2024). 'Strangers Meet We When' is concerned with the first meeting between Enid

Blyton and Royle's grandmother, Lola Onslow, who illustrated several of Blyton's fairy books in the early 1920s. The story originally appeared as the final section of *David Bowie, Enid Blyton and the Sun Machine* (Manchester University Press, 2023).

CHERISE SAYWELL was born and brought up in Australia. She has published two novels, *Desert Fish* and *Twitcher* (both Vintage). Her short stories have been broadcast on BBC Radio 4 and published in periodicals and anthologies including *Mslexia, A Short Affair* (Scribner) and *Bristol Short Story Prize Anthology* (Tangent Books). Her story 'Guests' was shortlisted for the BBC National Short Story Award in 2023. She lives in Edinburgh with her family.

KAMILA SHAMSIE was born and grew up in Karachi, Pakistan. She is the author of eight novels including *Burnt Shadows*, shortlisted for the Orange Prize, *A God in Every Stone*, shortlisted for the Women's Bailey's Prize and the Walter Scott Prize, and *Best of Friends*, shortlisted for the Indie Book Awards. Her seventh novel, *Home Fire*, won the Women's Prize for Fiction in 2018. It was also longlisted for the Man Booker Prize 2017, shortlisted for the Costa Best Novel Award, and won the London Hellenic Prize. Her story 'Churail' was shortlisted for the BBC National Short Story Award.

BEN TUFNELL is a writer and curator based in London. He has published widely on modern and contemporary art, in particular on artforms that engage with ideas of landscape and nature. His short stories have been published by *Conjunctions*,

Litro, *Lunate*, Nightjar Press, *Storgy* and *Structo*, amongst others. His debut novel, *The North Shore*, was published by Fleet (Little, Brown) in 2023.

CHARLOTTE TURNBULL's work has been published as part of the Galley Beggars Short Story Prize 2023, as well as by Nightjar Press, *New England Review*, *McNeese Review*, *Denver Quarterly*, *3:AM Magazine* and others.

CATE WEST is a writer, teacher, content designer and editor. She lives in the Midlands. Her MA in Creative Writing is from Manchester Metropolitan University, and she was 2022's Laura Kinsella Fellow at the National Centre of Writing. Her short fiction has been published by Nightjar Press, *Lunate*, *Janus Literary*, *Northern Gravy* and *The Amphibian*, among others. Her debut novel is on submission. Twitter: @c8west Agent: Charlotte Atyeo at Greyhound Literary.

ACKNOWLEDGMENTS

'Inside', copyright © Alan Beard 2023, was first published in *Thursday Nights: Short Fiction* (Tindal Street Fiction Group) curated by Rob Ganley, Alan Beard & Mick Scully, and is reprinted by permission of the author.

'Friday Art Club', copyright © Kevin Boniface 2023, was first published in *Sports & Social* (Bluemoose Books), and is reprinted by permission of the author.

'Manoeuvres', copyright © Paul Brownsey 2023, was first published in *Gutter* issue 27, February 2023, and is reprinted by permission of the author.

'The Sun is Only a Shipwreck Insofar as a Woman's Body Resembles It', copyright © Claire Carroll 2023, was first published in *Prototype 5* (Prototype Publishing) edited by Jess Chandler, Rory Cook & Aimee Selby, and is reprinted by permission of the author.

'Low Stakes', copyright © ECM Cheung 2023, was first published as *Low Stakes* (Loose Associations), and is reprinted by permission of the author.

Brian J Showers, and is reprinted by permission of the author.

'A Private Tutor', copyright © Gregory Norminton 2023, was first published in *Lunate* issue 3, and is reprinted by permission of the author.

'Strangers Meet We When', copyright © Nicholas Royle 2023, was first published in *David Bowie, Enid Blyton and the Sun Machine* (Manchester University Press), and is reprinted by permission of the author.

'Minor Disturbances', copyright © Cherise Saywell 2023, was first broadcast on BBC Radio 4, and is reprinted by permission of the author.

'Churail', copyright © Kamila Shamsie 2023, was first published in *Furies: Stories of the Wicked, Wild and Untamed* (Virago), and is reprinted by permission of the author.

'An Invocation', copyright © Ben Tufnell 2023, was first published in *New Ghost Stories IV* (The Fiction Desk) edited by Rob Redman, and is reprinted by permission of the author.

'Headshot', copyright © Charlotte Turnbull 2023, was first published online at *Galley Beggar Press Short Story Prize 2022/23*, 2023, and is reprinted by permission of the author.

'River', copyright © Cate West 2023, was first published online at *Fictive Dream*, and is reprinted by permission of the author.